Pasquale Festa Campanile
in 1957 with his novel *La nonna Sabella* which was published to great critical acclaim and won the Premio Re degli Amici and the Premio Corrado Alvaro. Since then he has published several books which have all been highly praised, including *Conviene far bene l'amore* and *Il ladrone,* Pasquale Festa Campanile was also well known for his work in the film industry and for screenplays written in collaboration with Massimo Franciosa. He died in February 1986.

For Love, Only for Love, winner of the Premio Campiello 1984, was first published in Italy by Bompiani under the title *Per amore, solo per amore.* It has been translated into English by William Weaver, highly acclaimed translator of *The Name of the Rose.*

For Love, Only For Love

Pasquale Festa Campanile

TRANSLATED BY

William Weaver

Futura

A Futura BOOK

Per amore, solo per amore was first published in Italy in 1984
by Gruppo Editoriale Fabbri, Bompiani Sonzogno, Etas S.p.A.,
Milan, Italy

First published in Great Britain in 1986 by
Macdonald & Co (Publishers) Ltd
London & Sydney

This edition published in 1987 by
Futura Publications, a Division of
Macdonald & Co (Publishers) Ltd

ISBN 0 7088 3236 9

Printed and bound in Great Britain by
The Guernsey Press Co. Ltd, Guernsey, Channel Islands.

Futura Publications
A Division of
Macdonald & Co (Publishers) Ltd
Greater London House
Hampstead Road
London NW1 7QX

A BPCC plc Company

1

The carpenters' guild of Galilee has asked me to write a reminiscence of our late member Joseph, inventor of a small but highly useful device, so that some notice of his life and his work will remain in the future. My suitability to this assignment is due to certain circumstances of which the first is my ability to read and write. The second is this: I was close to Joseph, as servant and I venture to say as friend, for the greater part of his life.

I will not have much to tell because Joseph's life was quite ordinary: he learned a trade, he married, he had a son. He also travelled, he went to Eygpt, but for reasons beyond his will; as soon as it was possible, he came back home.

Though I am less skilled with the pen than with the spoken word, I am glad to take up this job of writing because I approve the guild's decision. I believe that many people, besides me, would be happy if the name of the first man to make a spindle had been handed down, or that of the inventor of the pulley for lowering a bucket into a well: to know what sort of men they were, how they got the idea. There is something marvellous about inventing, similar to the act of creation. Something that does not exist comes into being, and from that moment on, it is as if it had always been.

When I met him, Joseph was eighteen, and I was about ten years older. As a consequence of certain adventures which I will not narrate, I had turned up in Bethlehem, in Judaea, with nothing but the tunic on my back. Without a penny, in other words. Moreover, Herod's soldiers were hunting for me because I bore a striking resemblance to a notorious chicken-thief, a petty robber of stables and farms. I could easily be taken for the man.

I found shelter in the shop of Ibrahim, an old carpenter, who took me on as his helper. This does not mean that he paid me, only that he was responsible for my safety and freedom. He was an Arab and he passed me off as his cousin. In reality, I am not an Arab, nor am I Jewish; and I am not a Galilean, either. I am thought to be Greek because my name is Socrates, but it would be hard for me to prove that I am or am not. I never knew my father or my mother.

Every afternoon a young man came to Ibrahim's shop, well-mannered, good-looking; and this, in fact, was Joseph. He did not seem serious, but rather one of those youths who want to learn a craft without making any effort; but, on the contrary, he worked hard and learned quickly, inspired by an authentic passion for the profession.

It was not long before I knew everything about him: he was the youngest son of a well-to-do farmer of the neighbourhood, the venerable Jacob, known also as 'Golden Tears', because he was always complaining, about the weather, about the poor season, the high price of seeds. And the more he wept, the more his farm seemed to flourish. Instead of sweating all day in the fields as his brothers did, Joseph had found a legitimate way to spend his afternoons in the shade.

Being a peasant was not for him. After he and I began to be close, which occurred very quickly, he would describe to me with revulsion the labour of the fields, the exhaustion, the monotony. 'The sweat of the brow,' he said, 'trickles through your lashes and stings your eyes; dust gets inside your tunic. You feel as if your own body doesn't belong to you; it's separated from you by a coat of salty water and earth.' He said also that, at a certain point, the spirit also abandons the brutalized limbs. Only the sensation of light on your eyelids remains, an incessant glare, the sun.

Escaping the sun, which sears fields and roads in summer, Joseph felt a sense of liberation. Besides, he liked wood: looking at it, touching it, breathing in the smell of freshly-hewn planks. He would doze off sometimes on the sawdust, its odour prompting sinful dreams.

How different men's tastes can be. Personally, I like the road, which marks off the land and gives us a different landscape at every turning. Old Ibrahim, known as 'Number One', not because he was an extraordinary man but because he was the first (and only) Arab to settle in the city, used to declare that in our work of carpentry there was primarily the pleasure of transforming inert wood, giving it a form, almost a life. According to Jacob nothing surpasses the joy of putting a seed in the ground and seeing a plant born from it. Joseph did not agree: he said that nature does everything on her own, and the peasant is only her servant. And so, like Ibrahim, he liked constructing any sort of object, pursuing his dream of inventing one that would be completely new.

When he felt so inclined, for his chief occupation was not learning the carpenter's craft, he spent a great deal of his time on girls: he would stand spellbound, holding the plane, and from his smile you could tell that he was thinking of Ruth or of Rebecca. I mention these two because, at that time, it was generally agreed that they were the most beautiful in the city; but there were also a number of others. Joseph dreamed of loving all the girls who thought about him. There were many, beautiful and ugly, even married women, prepared to run the risk of being stoned 'with stones neither too large nor too small', the official punishment for adulteresses.

Joseph was handsome with a head of dark curls, light skin, brown eyes. He reminded me of the statues of nude adolescents that I had seen in Greece and in other countries. In Judaea, where it was forbidden to paint or carve images because of the jealousy of God, the women could not call on such models to justify their admiration of Joseph. It was as if the young man coincided with a figure dreamed of but never encountered, with an ideal of beauty and love. He inspired a passionate and possessive tenderness, a lover's feelings, and a mother's.

I myself heard a serious person, the widow of the tax-collector, a lady mature in years and not easily moved, say to another woman, a friend, at the market: 'I would be ready to do anything with him, and I'm sure it wouldn't be a sin.' Spoken by a devout Jewish mother of four children, these words seemed to refer to a special innocence or inevitability in loving Joseph.

The same idea was expressed with equal succinct forcefulness by young Esther, daughter of Laban the tanner. Speaking of her desire to kiss Joseph, she said: 'I would like to kiss an angel, at least once.'

To other women the handsome Joseph suggested less spiritual images, but equally unexpected and innocent. A girl at the public washing tubs, Anna, daughter of Seth, saw him go by and said to the other girls: 'How pretty he is . . . tender and sweet . . . I could spread him on bread and eat him.' The girls of Bethlehem thought of him when they covered their bread with a light veil of honey in the morning, and they ate with increased appetite!

Towards evening, when Ibrahim was preparing to close the shop, Joseph and I would wash at the well in the courtyard. He would put on a fresh tunic, which he had brought from home, his good sandals, and would tie a little silk fillet around his head, before going out strolling. At times he would ask me to keep him company.

Perhaps because of the nearness of Jerusalem, a big city, holy and corrupt, behaviour in Bethlehem is not as strictly regulated as in other parts of Israel. A girl and a youth cannot walk in the street together, but it is permissible for them to meet for a moment at the well in the square, as she draws water and he stops to drink, (provided that everything seems random, not premeditated).

Joseph never failed to hover a few moments around the well. He replied with a smile to all the women who looked at him, even the old and the ugly, impartially; but each was left with the impression that she had attracted his gaze more than the others, that she had been enfolded in a warmer and more joyous greeting.

When he came out of Ibrahim's shop, Joseph turned the corner. He headed first for a position beneath the balcony of Ruth's house, or, to be more precise, across the street from it where there was a little belvedere and a young man could reasonably be supposed to have stopped to admire the view. The girl was already waiting, behind the curtain. The breeze lifted the cloth, widening the gap, and Ruth's dark hair could be seen. When she was outside, she concealed it beneath her kerchief.

Smiles were exchanged between street and balcony. A little string was lowered against the wall. Ruth, daughter of Jeremiah, couldn't write, and so she was sending her beloved a piece of cloth with a heart embroidered on it. The cloth was white; the heart, red. Joseph kissed Ruth's token, before hiding it among the folds of his tunic. The breeze swelled and raised the curtain. Ruth reached to seize the hem and draw the cloth in front of her. As she moved, her dress rose to her calf. A voice, heard inside, put an end to the meeting. The window was closed.

Joseph's image remained in her eyes, a sensation of joy transforming her face. She had entrusted herself symbolically to her beloved, and he had accepted her. Joseph didn't attach the same significance to Ruth's gesture. For him that heart was a message of love, not a commitment or a promise. He accepted it because he was a courteous youth, flattered that Ruth had declared herself first. Now he hastened down to the square, to the well, sure that Judith would be waiting for him there.

Judith, daughter of Nicodemus, was very different from the gentle Ruth. She was a wild girl, dishevelled in appearance. She spoke little, with a slightly hoarse voice. Her movements were abrupt; she used no colour on her cheeks. Though she wore very clean dresses, she was untidy. Put off by her haughtiness, all the young men of Bethlehem had to some extent succumbed to the girl's charms and had sought her love. Judith regularly humiliated them, loudly, in front of the women at the well. 'So,' she cried, 'you want to carry my pitcher home for me, and you'd kiss the ground I tread, eh? Well, that wish is easily satisfied. Here's the pitcher. Put it on your head and run to my house. And you there. This is a stone I stepped on. Come here, girls, watch Simeon kneel and kiss a stone!'

Simeon and his friend Judah suddenly remembered they had urgent business at the other end of the city, and they strode rapidly away. Indeed, some say the two youths actually ran. That same day Joseph vowed to himself that Judith would smile at him. She was so beautiful, the wild and aggressive girl, that it seemed a shame to him not to make her fall in love.

He had followed an ancient and foolproof system, trying to make her jealous. He had lavished smiles and courtesies on Rebecca, daughter of Hosea, a younger girl, skipping and smiling, who turned languid at his glances: Joseph, desired by all and considered unquestionably the most handsome, looked at her and spoke to her, filling her with content. Where all the other girls had sighed in vain, she had succeeded beyond all hope.

At least so it seemed. And so it seemed also to Judith, who

waited for Joseph after the bend in the road and, without lowering the pitcher from her head, ordered him: 'Leave her alone,' in that hoarse voice that made shivers run down the spine of the love-sick youths. 'Leave her alone. She's too young.'

'Who are you talking about?'

'Don't play the fool with me. *Rebecca*, the poor little creature,' and Judith, forgetting her pitcher, jerked her shoulder and her head towards the well. And the pitcher fell to the ground and broke. Joseph bent over to collect the shards. Exasperated, Judith aimed a kick at his behind, but he grabbed her ankle and pulled her down. They rolled on the ground, clinging to each other, growling; they seemed to be biting each other, but it was a kiss. They were barely in time to separate and recover their composure before the first girl appeared at the corner for news, having heard the crash of the pitcher.

After that the only thought in Judith's mind was to kiss Joseph or, as she put it, 'to devour him with kisses'. They kissed at night, when he climbed up the wall, pursing their lips so they could meet through the bars of the window, their noses bumping. They had hidden in an abandoned barn, in a wood shed, sniffed and pursued by dogs. They had climbed the great oak at the southern gate, but had had to retire because just at that hour, at sunset, the nocturnal birds nesting there left their homes, and the proud Judith was afraid of owls.

And Rebecca? Rebecca went on being happy, because Joseph had not stopped smiling at her. The other girl, Judith, understood immediately: everyone should believe that nothing had changed, they were all to see his smiles at the little one and to know nothing of the kisses Joseph gave her in secret.

So again this evening he went by the well, greeted the girls, smiled at Rebecca, filled her pitcher, then went on his way, taking the narrow lower road. Not much was left of the ancient fortifications: a tower, stones crumbling among the vegetable gardens. Only one patch of wall was still solid and intact, the stretch over the ravine. A rusted iron cage hung from the outer wall, uncovered, useless.

In it Joseph and Judith took refuge. Suspended over the void, clinging to each other, as the chain creaked and the cage threatened to come loose at any moment, the two kissed. That was all they did: the fear of God and of their neighbours restrained them. Their hands did not venture beneath their clothing, their legs hardly touched. But how exquisite were those caged kisses, secret and dangerous. Judith closed her eyes and saw herself condemned, with her beloved, to die in there, because she refused to succumb to the enemy and betray her people; she sank her lips into those of Joseph with desperate eagerness. Joseph pursued no heroic fantasies; he concentrated on sensations.

They did not stay there long: time for perhaps a dozen kisses, Judith calculated, but kisses that lasted, mingled one with the other, separated only by the need to catch a breath. Then the two of them came out, returned to this side of the wall: Judith went on to the well, and Joseph took the road that led out of the city, to his house among the fields. The day was not yet over. The sun was about to set behind the low hills to the west; trees and earth were changing colour. The sheep were returning towards the fold, after having been taken to graze far off, shepherded by the dogs and the children. This was the time when little Martha, daughter of Elijah, came home with her flock.

Joseph loved her slender little form, her big eyes, her pouting lips; but, even more, her untamed modesty, the bristling reserve with which she kept her suitors at bay. 'She doesn't have a good character,' the old women said of her, knowing the weapons with which a girl fights her way into a man's heart. But Joseph liked her: he thought that kissing her would be like biting a prickly fruit that defends its inner sweetness.

He appeared at her side, having waited for her behind a tree on a side path. They walked along, followed and surrounded by the sheep. Joseph greeted her first with a smile, with his charms as a proper young man. 'Go away,' she answered in one breath, frightened. Having a man beside her seemed an intolerable promiscuity to her.

'The road belongs to everybody,' Joseph replied. 'Are you telling me I have no right to use it?'

'But you are walking beside me.'

'What of that? If it displeases you that much, let me tell you that I am walking with your sheep. I can't even see you.'

'Go away. Or I'll turn the dog on you.'

'You wouldn't be that inhospitable.'

'Inhospitable?'

'Yes. Let's say that the stretch of road you're walking on belongs to you. Wouldn't you let me in, too, away from the weeds and the brush? Wouldn't you allow me to use your fine path of packed earth?'

Martha did not know what to answer; she was silent, blushing: hospitality is sacred and cannot be denied to anyone. She glanced at Joseph, who seemed amused by her embarrassment.

'Go away,' she said again, in a pleading voice, 'I don't want them to see me with you. Nobody's ever seen me with anybody.'

'Isn't it time you began? You can't live alone forever; your father and mother won't be enough for you after a while . . . '

They went on for a bit in silence, walking among the woolly sheep who, sensing that home was near, began to move faster. A distant call sounded among the fields and nearby, the sheep bleated, impatient to be milked.

Joseph did not like the sweetish odour of the flock. He liked the place, the hour, the sun at his back setting in an ocean of red clouds. But before him he saw faint colours, pinks and violets. The countryside spread out, down the hills, shorn and open; the great oaks and the terebinths were no longer green but bluish, already nocturnal trees. He was deeply aware of the person walking beside him; he felt the stirring in his spirit; Martha's determination to hold on to her innocence moved him.

She whispered: 'Joseph, why are you tormenting me?' and it was a sincere lament, not an argument. 'Joseph, why are you pressing me to be a woman? Don't you know I'm afraid?'

He touched her cheek with his fingertips, a rapid protective caress, and went off without saying goodbye to her. He called her from the distance, 'Martha,' and as she turned, he added: 'Don't you want me to be the one who torments you?' And he was implying it could have been another, any one of the young peasants from the area, an awkward and aggressive initiator, impelling her towards young womanhood.

Martha bowed her head, not answering. Joseph, as he went off, sensed that the moment had come, that the girl was about to lose her thorns: tomorrow, next week. Now there was no more haste.

He was trying to enter his father's house just as it was time to sit down at table. His brothers, Manasseh and Zebulon, were always so hungry after a day's work that they would fall on their food without saying a word. They were two coarse-featured boors: Manasseh had red hair, which grew an inch from his eyrbrows; Zebulon was shorter, dark and as wide as a cupboard, with curly hair and a cleft chin. Certainly they did not resemble Joseph. In the household, among the servants, there was talk that the youngest of the brothers was the son of a Phoenician slave-girl whom old Jacob had loved very much: this would explain the father's preference for the boy and the lack of resemblance between Joseph and the other two.

The old man, too, once the prayer was said, did not utter a word. He sensed clearly the tension that poisoned things among the young men seated before him. Manasseh (and also Zebulon who always followed his older brother in everything) considered it an insult, seeing Joseph come to the table all fresh and clean, with a linen tunic and fine sandals, his hair neatly combed, and the joy of life bubbling in him, however suppressed beneath his serious manner and his sober demeanour. In tacit protest, the oldest son did not wash before eating, and neither did Zebulon, thus rousing wrath in Jacob's heart. One of these days Golden Tears would assuredly drive them from his sight: they stank and they did not pray and purify themselves, as was right, before approaching their food.

Manasseh looked with hatred at Joseph, because the youngest brother worked in the fields as little as possible and their father let him have his way, because he had success with girls, because he was handsome and polite. Manasseh would also have had other things to hold against the youth but he did not yet know them. Nor did Joseph, for it had only been in the past few days that Manasseh had begun to think of the widow Tamar, and he had not yet told anyone about it. And so, after eating, Joseph pretended he was retiring to his room, but, instead, he jumped from the window and returned to the city. Furtively, he stole along the mill road towards Tamar's house, looking around. His caution was not due to any fear of Manasseh, since he was unaware of his brother's aspirations to the widow. He enjoyed imagining all sorts of dangers, to enhance the pleasure of this adventure. At this hour of the night there was never anyone out, but Joseph had put on his sandals of palm bark so as to make no noise as he walked over the cobbles.

Tamar's house was a rather large building, set towards the road. Joseph entered through a little gate which stood open, and hurried along a narrow walk, paved with stones. To his left was the side of the house; to his right, the shadows of the vegetable garden. Though there was a moon, as he walked along the wall, under the cover of the boughs of the trees Joseph was well hidden. He stopped below a familiar window, which seemed closed but was open; he grabbed the sill and pulled himself up. For a moment the white patch of his tunic could be seen, then he spun around and was at once beyond, in the perfumed darkness.

In the Scriptures venerated by the children of Israel it is said that Esther was steeped in perfumes for a full year before she was presented to the king: nard, cinnamon, anis, myrrh. Tamar had been sprinkling her skin with aromatic essences for at least ten years, assuming she began the care of her person at fifteen. Big, white, lazy, the widow spent almost all her time lying down and she had a tendency to put on weight; her remedy for this was a series of purges that lasted ten days, during which time Tamar would see no one. Easy, smooth, highly perfumed, Tamar was rather stupid, a quality Joseph found becoming and charming in her.

She had noticed Joseph a month before. She had drawn him into the house with an excuse, as the youth had clearly understood, when she called him from behind the door: 'Come in,' she had said, 'a fox has got into the house and I can't get rid of it.' The fox was found at once, a stuffed fox, in one of the ground-floor rooms opening on to the central court; but Joseph's seduction was carried out in the upper room, built on the terraced roof where the nights were more cool and the moon could be seen through the light curtains drawn from one corner to the other.

That is where Joseph climbed up every night afterwards. He reached the roof and with an anticipatory smile, he approached the drawn curtains.

Joseph was happy to lie with Tamar, but he would never have taken advantage of any of the other young girls who buzzed around him.

He knew that if they were to be caught in sin, the consequences would be immediate and terrible while Tamar, a rich widow with no relatives or ties, ran no risk. With Ruth, with Judith, and the others, he did not feel he was doing anything wrong: it was all a game they were playing together, as they entered youth. The idea that one or all of the girls would fall so in love with him that she would suffer if he left her one day barely crossed his mind. It was so beautiful to feel them near, to see them, kiss them; and Joseph went no further.

Still he took care that one did not learn of another; but even this was not wickedness: it was a part of the game. One was not enough for him; he wanted them all, and there was no other way. It seemed cruel to him not to reply to a glance with a smile, not to accept the silent offer that this or that girl made him of her sighs. Then, once matters had proceeded, it would have been a crime to sadden the girl by informing her of how things stood.

And so he perfected his understanding with five or six girls, none of whom suspected that she had a rival. And, in Joseph's view, all of them were happy. He himself, sated by the embraces of Tamar, could treat them gaily and politely, with none of the sadness caused by thwarted desire.

II

I have reported the words and actions of Joseph belonging to those moments when he was in a girl's company, and I have done this confidently and precisely as if I had also been present. Since I will have to proceed in this way more than once in the course of my narrative, I wish to make it clear that I have invented nothing. To the curious man few things remain hidden. I followed Joseph day after day. I discovered all his intrigues; on Tamar's roof, flattened in the shadows beneath the low wall that enclosed the terrace, I too, was often present. Some details were recounted to me by reliable persons, tales and tears of betrayed girls have been poured out to me. Joseph himself sometimes confessed thoughts and aims that he never confided in anyone else. Where there was a gap in my information, I went ahead through deduction, but I rarely had need of it.

The reason why I always wanted to know everything about Joseph is quickly explained. As I have said before, I am naturally curious, one of those itching, pushy busybodies who can never be still unless they have thoroughly investigated what interests them. In this case my eagerness was stimulated by the fact that I had chosen Joseph as my master. He did not agree: not only because he had nothing to pay me with, but also because giving orders was uncongenial to him.

As far as my pay was concerned, I told him not to worry: it would be enough for him to give me what Ibrahim gave me, namely nothing. Besides, I would not guarantee him obedience: there were many circumstances in which I liked to behave in my own fashion. What I was really proposing to him was a partnership, a little union that lay somewhere between friendship and mutual aid, in which I would play the role of the servant somewhat casually, as Joseph would casually play the role of master.

In him I admired many qualities that I had lost: good will, good faith, a readiness to believe in others and to love them. Joseph did not want me near him always, but he would have walked a full day to find a medicine for me.

A series of events finally linked my lot with his: I became his servant and partner, and he accepted me because he could not have rejected me.

A complicated web like the one Joseph was weaving with his girls is always on the point of breaking. If a single thread snaps, then the whole net comes undone.

Joseph had continued carrying inside his tunic the red heart that Ruth had embroidered for him. It seemed to keep him warm, to reassure him. One evening he took off his belt in order to kiss Judith more comfortably in the iron cage, and the piece of cloth slipped to his feet, flapped for a moment on one of the bars, then dropped, spinning, to the bottom of the ravine. Joseph saw it, but he thought Judith had not noticed and, in any case, would never go down there to look for it, amid the nettles and refuse.

Judith said nothing; the next day she went to rummage at the foot of the drop and she found it. She understood immediately what the heart meant, and she began yelling and grinding her teeth until, after she had unburdened herself, she could climb up again, with her old mood restored, mettlesome but calm. Now it was a question of discovering who her rival was. Judith carried out the enquiry in a manner all her own: she would suddenly pull out the cloth heart in front of this or that girlfriend and await the reaction. Ruth flushed, then paled. As Judith towered over her, hands on her hips, the girl promptly admitted that Joseph was the man she loved: 'And he loves me, too, so what's wrong about that?'

'Has he ever kissed you?' Judith asked.

'No, I wouldn't have let him.'

'Has he at least tried to kiss you?'

To this question, too, Ruth was forced to answer no. The other girl did not feel the least bit consoled: this love without kisses seemed dangerous to her. According to Ruth, she and Joseph had never met alone; he had spoken to her on occasion, no more than a greeting, at the well, in everyone's presence.

'In that case, how can you say he loves you, silly?'

Ruth examined in her heart the reasons for her selfconfidence, and said innocently: 'By the way he smiled at me. Nobody smiles at a girl like that unless he loves her. And besides, he took the heart that I threw down to him and he put it inside his tunic, over his own heart. And now you talk: tell me why you stole it from him? You're envious, a jealous trouble-maker!'

Judith, who had already had more than enough to put up with that day, gave her a slap. They fought, there on the spot, at the corner of the road. And since Ruth shouted at the other girl to leave Joseph alone, they promptly found a third girl who protested because she believed herself to be the only one, the true love of Joseph, who talked to her, hidden among the branches of a carob, beneath her window. Instead of joining in the quarrel, Zora, daughter of Gaber, a quick-thinking girl, invited the other pair to come to her house and hold council.

'How can we share him?' the argumentative Judith said in her usual brusque tone. Though she had discovered that Joseph's kisses were reserved for her alone, or perhaps for this very reason, she felt the most betrayed.

Zora set a glass of anis-water before her, as refreshment. 'First of all,' she said sagely, 'let's see how many there are to share him.'

The idea – the suspicion, that is – came into the minds of the other two for the first time. They established a plan of action. If they assumed that Joseph was after more than one girl, then his conquests had to be sought among the young and beautiful ones. They made up a list. Whenever one of the three of them happened to meet a girl on the list, they would bring up the subject of Joseph.

They followed their plan, and the name of Joseph, suddenly produced in the midst of idle chatter, prompted revealing reactions. Thus they discovered that Rebecca was one of their number, and they found another girl or two. The betrayed spread into the countryside and added poor Martha to their group, that evening as she came home with her flock, the child who had barely begun to pay heed to Joseph.

They gathered in Zora's garden and plotted their revenge.

Sweet Rebecca hesitated. She defended him: 'After all, he's

done nothing bad. You, Judith, say he's betrayed us all, but that's not so. He smiled at us, he even kissed you, but he didn't promise anything to any of us. He didn't even say he loved us. At least,' she concluded, blushing, 'he never said it to me.'

'Obviously, he hasn't yet made up his mind; he's waiting to choose,' Ruth added, thinking of Joseph beneath her window, Joseph with the silken fillet in his hair knotted over one ear, with those muscles that tautened his tunic at the shoulders and across his chest, with that spell-binding smile. Standing there, his caressing eyes looking up, his head bent slightly to one side, Wasn't his whole attitude perhaps a declaration and a promise? The girl shivered, looked at the others around her, the ones to whom Joseph had addressed the same attentions, whom he had lured only so that he could mock them, perhaps boast about them to the other youths, his friends. She, too, voted for revenge.

They separated, with the understanding that each would work out a plan on her own. They conceived some highly ingenious ways of punishing Joseph. One suggested catching him at the public bath with the complicity of the attendants, covering him with tar, and then goose-feathers. Another, more fierce, wanted him to be whipped. Judith proposed that they should capture him, all together, rip off his tunic, and put a woman's dress on him, then force him to cross the square on market-day. They would cover him with such shame that he would have to leave the city for good!

Rebecca was the last to speak. 'None of you knows anything yet. Can you guess who the woman is that Joseph visits at night? Not to chat, but to make love, like a husband with a wife?'

Amid the general consternation she told about the affair with Tamar, which she had discovered herself, spying at night from the widow's garden. From her house she could see everything, when there was a moon. Rebecca was unable to sleep, thinking of how Joseph had betrayed her; she went up on the roof to find some cool air and one night she thought she could see him, stealing into Tamar's house like a thief, climbing in at a window. Was it Joseph, or wasn't it? Then he came out on Tamar's roof, and it was Joseph, beyond any doubt. Tamar was awaiting him in the airy room with the white curtains.

They laughed. Rebecca could not see a great deal, her house being an arrow's flight from that other, with the garden between. But she clearly recognized the forms outlined behind the curtains, and it was not hard for her to guess what the pair was up to.

'Did you watch everything?' the unschooled Martha asked, blushing.

The other girl answered yes, but actually she had immediately gone back down to her room, upset and ashamed.

Curiously, the new revelation redirected a part of the resentment that the girls felt, from Joseph's head to Tamar's. She was the seductress, the hussy; she was the true rival. Joseph sought the love of the girls to elude the widow's spell, to have the strength to leave her. All agreed on this interpretation of the events. First they had to set Joseph free, help him recover himself; then they would decide. He deserved punishment but that woman was surely more responsible, and they had to take vengeance on her rather than on him. For Tamar the good girls thought of fierce punishments which would make up for those spared Joseph. They dreamed of shaving her head, disfiguring her, pouring a cauldron of boiling water on her. They released their anger, piling cruelty upon cruelty. Then, partially appeased, but still vexed and suffering, they pondered more moderate and possible acts of revenge.

On leaving Ibrahim's shop that evening, I told Joseph I had to speak with him, and instead of going towards the square, I led him into the country. He listened scrupulously to the news that I gave him: the girls knew everything, they had decided to avenge themselves.

Unfortunately there was a second piece of news that I should have communicated to Joseph, but I could say nothing, because I did not know it. It concerned his brothers. They know of his intrigue with Tamar. As the prudent widow was keeping Manasseh in suspense, answering neither yes nor no to his proposals, the older man felt insulted that Joseph had been preferred to him; and he was furious. Manasseh, known as Anvil, because as a child he had accidentally been struck on the head with a hammer, was a bit slow in having ideas and, when he was faced by an adversary, most of the time settled matters with his fists.

I suggested to Joseph that he keep clear of Tamar's house, at least for a while.

'Tonight I have to go,' he insisted, 'at least to let her know.'

'I can go . . . '

Joseph looked at me with a smile, which was enough to discourage me. I am not a man Tamar would ever listen to, being a foreign infidel.

Joseph was resting, supine, on Tamar's bed; he had one hand on the back of the widow, who had fallen asleep beside him. Outside there was a great silence. Every now and then dogs barked in the courtyards; restless hens woke for mysterious reasons, infected other hens with their own uneasiness, and together they all clucked and stretched their wings for a moment. Then silence again: a footstep on the road would be heard at a great distance . . . Unless someone were approaching barefoot or keeping to the verges, thick with grass . . . .

The scent of myrtle and jasmine rose up from the garden, joining other scents breathing in the love chamber.

Joseph came through the gate before dawn and, having crossed it, plunged into a darker, stifling night. They had tied a cloak over his head. They carried him far off, to beat him at their convenience, where his cries would wake no one. They climbed a narrow path that led out of the city, towards the hill.

There were two of them, silent so as not to be recognized; but Joseph could guess their identity from the stink of stable and sweat. He could not help but call them by name: 'Zebulon, Manasseh, put me down.'

They did put him down, but only to start kicking him and beating him until Joseph no longer had the strength to move. Whenever he came to and began to writhe inside the cloak, they would resume hitting him. This was repeated three times, until they finally dumped him in a hedge bristling with thorns. Rolling out of it, when the pair had gone off, was even more of a torture. Luckily the widow's house was not too distant, and Joseph could drag himself there before the city awoke.

Tamar tended him, removing one thorn after another with gentle hands, kissing him and weeping. She stopped just to go down to the square for a moment to buy some aloes, which, mixed with wine, make a very effective unguent.

In the square, her agitation was taken for sinful dishevelment: the disorder of her dress (her tunic opened to her thigh) was to be put down to her haste and was interpreted as a provocation by the girls at the well. Four of the seven were there, but they impulsively made the decision for their missing friends. What was the use of waiting and constructing complicated vengeances? They exchanged a look, a nod of agreement, then took the dumbfounded Tamar and flung her into the water so quickly that they had time to get away before people realized what had happened.

Tamar screamed and wept in a fit of hysterics, which succeeded in causing precisely what she had *not* wanted: a scandal. As she finally climbed out of the water, her tunic sticking to her body, she was an object of curiosity (and of desire among the men present). An inquisitive murmuring ran through the people; they wondered who had treated Tamar like that, and why.

The women became aware that the widow wanted to go home alone and insisted they should let her go. Joseph came down to the door, trying to get out before the little procession could discover him in the house; but he had left it too late. He appeared on the threshold barefoot, still bleeding, a sheet wrapped around him.

It was no longer a scandal: it was the event of the year, all the more fascinating for its mystery. All Bethlehem talked of nothing else.

Joseph could no longer go home. He did not want to avenge himself, but simply wanted never to see his brothers again, to erase them even from his memory. He moved to the inn, determined not to go out for a while, not even during the day. As for the widow, she would not have left her house for a gold talent. Joseph had been forced to confess to her that he had been toying with seven girls at the same time, kissing only one regularly and another, Zora, from time to time. Under different circumstances Tamar would have been greatly amused by this story, as she would have been proud of being the only one, of the many, to enjoy the favours of the much-desired youth. Now she had suffered outrage, with all the ensuing gossip, and it was too wounding. She gladly agreed that Joseph should move to a safe and neutral place.

'What if I went away?' Joseph asked me, when I went to pay him a visit. At the inn he was bored, or rather, he missed the usual features of life, the dusty roads, the countryside, Ibrahim's shop, the wood there, his craft.

'Where shall we go?' I automatically joined him: if he left, he would not succeed in leaving me behind.

The inn was uncomfortable; Joseph had eaten and slept better at his house. He was a lazy youth, but forced idleness depressed him. He sat for hours under the pergola, where the hay was piled and where the asses and mules were curried. The great rectangular yard was surrounded by stalls and arcades on two sides; on the third there were some low buildings where travellers were lodged. The fourth side was empty, with iron rings set in the wall, where mounts and work-animals were tied. In the open space there were wagons, barrels, sacks and baskets under a shed; in the centre, a well.

Joseph, when he had eaten supper, came out into the yard. We sat in a dark corner, listening to the words of the camel-drivers and the servants.

'Socrates,' he asked me, 'is travel a fine thing, in your opinion?'

I had never walked from one place to another on a whim, I explained, but out of necessity: travelling is an art, painful and difficult like any other. The roads are full of dangers: storms, floods, but most of all, brigands, thieves, murderers, mercenaries, runaway slaves, thieving nomads, fierce mendicants or even peaceful peasants, who hide in the bushes and cut the throat of the solitary wayfarer.

Joseph began polishing a piece of wood, something that can be done also in the dark. I brought him a series of tools, at his request. He said he had to work at something; otherwise he had no appetite. To tell the truth, he did not work much; he did not make a chair or a stool; he only sawed the trunk of a young cypress, making some discs that could be set under goblets, but he cut them of equal thickness and polished them and filed them until they were perfect circles. He loved his craft; he liked doing even the smallest things well.

We stayed in our corner, sitting on the ground, in silence. That is to say, we were quiet, but around us that constant stirring could be heard that continues until night has fallen completely, in a place with many inhabitants: the chatting of people drinking in one of the ground-floor rooms, the stifled cries of dice-players, the soft calls of the servants, the restless animals in their stalls striking the mangers and the wooden columns.

'Instead, why don't you marry one of them?' I suggested to him. 'You have seven to choose from. Tell me which one you want. I'll send the marriage-broker to your father, and everything will be arranged. Your brothers will leave you in peace; the girls will calm down. You go back home to live, you settle down. Or else your father gives you enough money to set up a carpenter's shop of your own.'

Joseph answered me: 'When you take one, you lose all the others. Marriage isn't just the end of youth; to me it seems the end of life itself. How is it possible to give up all the beauties that swarm around us? Why should I forbid myself tomorrow to smile at Ruth and at Rebecca, because I'm married to Martha? When one of them looks at me in a certain way,' he continued, in a low voice, 'I feel a heat in my wrists, my mind clears, I want to laugh and I want her to laugh with me and tell me that life is beautiful. Girls are the joy of the world.'

As we conversed, we approached the lighted part of the yard, where the glow fell from a lantern suspended from a pole. Joseph held up the saw and cut his branch into little circular slices. A little girl of seven or eight came from the inner rooms, all alone, eluding her parents' guard; she came to investigate. She looked at Joseph with admiration, as if she were seeing one of those princes in fairy-tales. She tugged at the hem of his tunic. 'I'm thirsty,' she said.

Joseph was always polite with any member of the female sex, from little girls to old women, even the ugly ones. He put down the saw, pulled the rope of the well, dipped a glass into the bucket, and handed it to her. People usually start a conversation with a child by asking its name. She forestalled him: 'What's your name?'

'Joseph.' A smile, a little bow: my master was incurable; he employed his charm almost without being aware of it. Then he also introduced me, quite superfluously: 'This is Socrates.' She gave me a brief glance, then ignored me, as a subject unworthy of her interest. I do not like people to ignore me, so I spoke to her: 'And what is your name?'

'Maria.' And she added, putting me in my place: 'I don't like you.'

I would not dwell on this encounter, a trivial and ordinary incident, if the child were not destined to occupy a certain place in Joseph's life, and also in mine.

For the moment she was no one, even if Joseph was not insensible to her admiration. He asked her questions, petted her, bent over her and crouched until his head was at the same level as hers. Maria answered in a few words, then gradually freed herself of her shyness and also chatted freely. Her voice was faint, a chirping like a baby chick's, you would say; she emitted a sharp and mournful cry, raising her head and sniffing at the same time. She was comical.

'And what are you doing here alone?'

'I'm not alone. I've come from Nazareth with my uncle and aunt. We're going to visit Aunt Elizabeth, near Jerusalem. Her husband's a priest.'

As she spoke, she broke off every now and then to emit her little bird-like squeak. I knew so little about children that it was a moment before I realized: Maria had the hiccups. Her skin and hair were dark; she was a bit dishevelled, thin, with protruding shoulder-blades. Stubborn, serious for her age, she was determined to exclude me and, in fact, she then asked Joseph: 'And what are you doing here alone?'

'I'm waiting.'

'What for?'

'I don't know.'

Maria looked at him almost with pity: obviously the young man needed someone who would make decisions for him. How could he spend his days waiting, without knowing what for? I believe I can interpret the development of her ideas because she then asked him: 'Are you married?' In my opinion, she was mentally suggesting herself as someone capable of taking care of him and guiding him. When Joseph said he wasn't, she continued her investigation: 'Are you engaged?' Again Joseph said no.

Finally the little thing smiled: until then she had looked at him intensely, frowning. Now, relieved, she stopped behaving like an adult. She began playing with Joseph. She picked up the discs of cypress that he had sawed. 'What are these?'

'Whatever you want them to be: wheels, for example.'

Joseph rolled one over the compact earth of the yard as a demonstration. Immediately Maria cried: 'Let me try!' Her disc fell on its side after a couple of cubits. She did not give up, but tried once more. As I said: she was stubborn. Again the disc wobbled and fell.

'Why won't it stand up?' the child complained.

'You really want the wheel to stay up? Then it takes four of them.'

Maria watched in wonder as Joseph's hands sawed and drilled, sticking the little wheels on to two iron rods, which he then fixed to a piece of flat wood. In other words, he built a little cart, no more than three inches off the ground. A little string tied to the two ends of the front axle allowed it to be steered.

In one part of the vast yard Joseph found a suitable slope and showed the child how to ride down fast, his knees bent.

'Now I'll try.'

Joseph did not suggest that she crouch beside him, expressed no apprehension, no warning to be careful. And Maria, with a cry of delight, steered her humble coach down the incline. She carried it up again and started again. She had never had such a plaything, a male game. She wriggled with joy in a fever of excitement, spellbound, proud of herself. She was a beautiful little girl, tall, quick. Behind her shy and tender appearance she had a brave spirit and a powerful will.

They called her from inside, and Maria, very reluctantly, broke off her playing. She went over to Joseph, pulling the cart, and handed him the string.

'Keep it; it's yours,' he said.

Maria could hardly believe it: this marvellous vehicle would be hers from now on; she swelled with gratitude. She went towards the door, waving goodbye with one hand, as she pulled the cart along with the other. Then she came back and put something in Joseph's hand. First, she hesitated, as if the act were costing her an effort, then she made up her mind and bestowed the gift with a smile. It was a little polished stone, rose-coloured with fine yellow veins. Joseph held it in his hand for a long time before he put it in his pocket.

III

I had also moved to the inn, where I slept outside Joseph's room, on the floor, to make certain he would not go away without me. I begged with my master to stir himself, to take some initiative.

'There's no need,' he would answer. 'Something will happen, and I'll act accordingly.'

Finally something did happen: his father sent for him. Joseph, dressed in his finest clothes, went to the house in broad daylight, at the very hour when people go home to eat. I walked a pace behind him, as his escort.

In the old house there was no one to be seen, except for the serving-maids. During the fine weather, the men, including Joseph's brothers, stayed out in the fields, stopping their work only long enough to eat a mouthful in the shade of a tree. Jacob sat down at the table alone with his favourite son, while I made myself comfortable in the kitchen.

The old man sighed, tears running down his cheeks. Joseph realized it was a farewell, and a fear of the future and of the unknown gripped his heart.

'Leave here, to spare yourself and others occasions of sin,' Jacob said. 'God knows what I suffer, letting you go away like this, depriving myself of the consolation of my old age; but I firmly believe I am acting for your own good. There will be no peace in this house as long as you are here, to stir up your brothers' envy. I know you have undergone violence at their hands.'

Joseph also started crying. For the first time, in eighteen years of his life, he would have to fend for himself, alone. Jacob gave him a purse of money, his share of the inheritance. Then he put his hand on the boy's head. 'May the Lord guide your steps and bless your actions,' he said, and his voice quivered.

He must have had to think about it a long time, before making that decision. To separate himself from Joseph cost him a great sacrifice, for this was the only son in whom he recognized himself; but the family had to go on, the farm had to produce, the flocks and herds had to increase. Jacob wanted to keep his sons from destroying one another, or rather to save Joseph from the brutality of his brothers. He wanted no dramas; in old age, dramas are a terrible nuisance.

We went back to the city while the sun was still high. Joseph was dejected, and I had to take care of all the preparations for our departure. I even remembered to go to Tamar's house, by the back way, and take her my master's farewell. I bought an ass, and I made ready two tall cornel-wood staves, the support of the wayfarer. Joseph asked me also to provide a complete set of carpenter's tools. A couple of bundles and some provisions completed our luggage.

The greatest burden consisted of the purse of money. Although relatively small, we did not know where to put it. It seemed to me that wherever we hid it, it was all too obvious. In Joseph's opinion we should not worry: the next morning a group of merchants was setting off, bound for Jaffa, on the sea, and we would join them. The party was protected by an armed, mounted escort; we would pay our share to the merchants and could then travel safely.

But then, to bolster his courage, Joseph stayed up drinking the night before, and rose late the next morning, after the merchants' caravan had already left. When we had loaded the ass and put on our hob-nailed travelling sandals, we set off at the hottest hour of the day. Since we had to cross the town, my master preferred this time, when everyone was in the house resting; no one would see us. The ass went first, with me holding his halter; Joseph walked on his own, his head bowed. He was certainly thinking of the girls he had deceived and who had not chosen to take their revenge on him. The fact that he would never see them again was punishment enough: Judith of the searing kisses, Ruth with her cloth heart, the tender Rebecca, Martha among her sheep, and the others, all of them very dear.

He raised his eyes to Ruth's window: a white veil flapped to say goodbye to him, held beyond the bars by a little, dark hand. Joseph undid the fillet that bound his hair and replied with the same gesture. A red kerchief greeted Joseph at Judith's window. The girls had learned that their prince was leaving. Not only those he had deluded, but also the others, the too young and the old, the married and the ugly: all of them made gestures of farewell. Veils, girdles, shawls of every colour waved from almost every window. On that sultry day when not a breath of air was stirring, it was a surprising sight to see all those feminine banners fluttering like wings, in silence.

We left the town and walked for a long time without speaking. I, too, was sad to leave the city that had given me refuge for months; I, too, had said goodbye that night to a girl, a servant like me, a foreigner like me, who washed the pots at the inn, no less deserving of regret than the girls Joseph was leaving.

We took the road for Jerusalem. The night before Joseph had insisted on leaving the heavy purse of money on the ass with the rest of our baggage. In his view, thieves and bandits would never look for the purse among the carpenter's tools and our linen. But I suffered at the thought that the money was separated from us, exposed to the whim of an animal, who might run off and hide among the trees on the hills.

'Then you carry it,' Joseph decided, thus giving me a proof of his trust and charging me with a great responsibility. At first I refused, but as he insisted, I divided the contents of the purse among the inner pockets of a leather belt, which I fastened around my waist.

Towards evening, at a last curve, we found ourselves before Jerusalem, 'like a stag reclining upon the hills'. Our road flanked the tower of David and the palace of Herod, which Joseph had already seen once, when he had come to the temple for Passover. But my master did not know the lower city with its maze of little streets and alleyways, that climb up and down, some turning into steps; the houses huddled against one another; the smell (of food, of refuse, of meat burned in sacrifices), and the noise (of criers, marching soldiers, smiths, pilgrims, pedlars, animals being led to the temple) that fills the air. He did not like it; he felt stifled there, regretting the open space and the pure air of his town.

We found room at an inn, not far from the Fountain of the Virgin, after we had crossed the whole city.

That evening, as we were seeking relief from the heat, sitting on the terrace-roof of the inn, Joseph told me his plans: we would head north, towards Galilee, which is the land named by Exodus, where milk and honey flow, the first that the children of Israel reached, fleeing the tyranny of the Pharaohs. From somewhere in Galilee came the heavy ears of corn and the long bunches of grapes that the young warriors, sent ahead in the vanguard, brought back to Moses.

'And what will you do in Galilee?'

'I'll be a carpenter,' Joseph answered.

'Why? You don't lack for money.'

'I will be a rich carpenter,' he decided, laughing.

His fondness for the craft was deep, especially because he was good at it. Working in wood was his calling. His satisfaction, on looking at an object produced by his hands - a bench, a table, a coffer, which had been only planks and pieces of wood a short time before - revealed in him the true artisan.

'And besides,' Joseph concluded, 'money is here today and gone tomorrow, but a craft remains always. Am I right?'

We went downstairs. He retired to a room, where he was to sleep with two other travellers, and I headed for the stables, to sleep with the ass.

I woke before the sun had appeared, and I rolled over on the straw, with a sensation of lightness: I was on the road again, with no worries about food and lodging. I had my health; there was money. Money! I let out a cry. The leather belt was no longer around my waist, as it had been when I lay down to sleep. I searched desperately in my pallet, then in the straw of the animals. I found the belt, but it was empty; they had cut it with a knife and slipped it off me as I slept.

I didn't know how to break the news to Joseph; all his plans and mine had plunged into the void. I appeared before him, holding the cut belt in my hand; and I breathlessly told him the terrible news. Among other things, I was afraid he might suspect me. He let me wait a long time for a word from him, then he said, 'Did you look for the thief?'

'No,' I answered, shaking my head; I knew that the guilty man would already be far away.

'Look for him,' Joseph ordered, with a severity I had never seen in him before. He let me roam all day between stables and inn-yard, asking this one and that for news of the gold. Then, when it was dark, he called me.

'Does everyone know now,' he asked me, in a reproachful tone, 'that we had a lot of money and it was all stolen from you, down to the last penny?'

'I couldn't do any searching without telling what I was searching for.'

'I'm not reproaching you, Socrates. Everything's fine. Now nobody will think of robbing us.'

I didn't know which to admire more, his philosophical indifference to the loss of the money or his indulgence towards me. We set off again the next morning: in dealing with the landlord Joseph suffered because, unable to pay, he had to leave a fine new cloak with the man instead.

That day we dug into the scant provisions we had brought along with us. Towards evening, when it was past the hour for travellers to get off the roads because of the gathering darkness and take shelter in inns and taverns or camp in large groups around the fire, we were attacked by four ugly ruffians armed with swords and mounted on racing camels. I was preparing to put up a fierce resistance, using my pilgrim's staff; but Joseph said: 'We have no money, brothers; we have already been robbed, in Jerusalem.'

The leader of the four started laughing. 'It's that pair from the inn of the Virgin: completely cleaned out. We needn't waste our time with these wretches.' He gave me a blow on the back with the flat of his sword and rode off with the others, still laughing.

'You see?' Joseph remarked, with a pleased look. 'The rumour spread.'

I did not understand why he was so pleased, and I asked him.

'I'll tell you,' he answered, but he did not start speaking until we had lighted a fire in a little olive grove and were eating some dried figs and hard biscuit, all that was left of our supplies. There was a beautiful inn a stone's throw away, but we couldn't allow ourselves even to enter it: travellers without money are treated worse than dogs.

'I know,' Joseph said, as if he were resuming an interrupted tale, 'that some hot broth and a glass of wine would cheer this meal, which is as sad as a man without money . . . Do you think they would give you either, if you went to the inn and asked?' And he pointed to the lighted windows and the fire burning in the yard.

'Of course,' I answered, 'if, along with my request, I handed them a silver piece.'

I thought I had deflated him, but on the contrary, Joseph smiled. 'Try this,' he said, holding out a gold daric. 'See that they weigh it carefully and give you fair change,' he added.

It was one of the gold pieces that old Jacob had put in the purse, along with more recent Greek and Roman pieces and with coins minted in this country, which bear no human images and can be used to pay the obol due to the God of Israel. I was so stunned that I didn't dare ask for any explanations. I ran to the inn with a pan and a pitcher, and came back with broth, wine, and a number of silver and copper coins, which were my change.

'Are you sure no one followed you?' Joseph asked me, sipping the broth.

The night was very bright, but in the olive grove a thief could have hidden, one who had seen me change the gold piece and wanted to discover where I kept the others. Joseph stood up and we moved out of the shadow of the olives into the middle of a large, bare meadow. There we were visible, but we ourselves would have seen from a distance anyone who approached.

'Do you understand now why you would never have found the thief who stole the purse?' Joseph asked me.

I hadn't understood a thing and I answered, sincerely: 'No.'

'Because I am the thief,' Joseph said, in the tone of someone anticipating applause. Seeing the fury in my eyes, he hastened to add: 'I didn't warn you, otherwise you wouldn't have been convincing when you had to act the part of the victim. Forgive me. You've seen the result: the rumour has spread, and the thieves pay no attention to us.'

I could have killed him. I mean it: in the past I had fought for much less. But I realized the cleverness of the trick my master had devised, and I admired the cool way he had carried out his plan, despite my desperation.

Where was the money? Where it should have been from the beginning, in the ass's pack. My master had thrust it down to the bottom of the box of nails, where a thief would never find it, unless he emptied the whole cask. But why would a thief ever want to remove the nails from a cask?

There was a weak point in Joseph's reasoning about the money, the nails, and the cask, but a bit of time had to go by before he became aware of it. In easy stages, following the road up and down the hills, we had arrived at the city of Schechem in Samaria. Because of the way he had been brought up, Joseph distrusted Samaritans, who broke away from the people of God and built a temple of their own on Mount Gerizim; but he was not indifferent to the smiles of the Samaritan women, nor were they able to resist his.

We set off again one morning at dawn and, after having walked till midday, we began to look for a cool spot to eat and rest. We saw a cluster of houses, a little village, on our left; and we headed in that direction.

'May the Lord be with you,' Joseph said to a woman who was looking over a little wall at the street, 'is there an inn or a tavern in this village?'

'There are no taverns here, foreigner,' she replied, 'but you can tie your ass to the iron bars of the gate and come into my garden with your servant to rest.'

The woman was beautiful, the garden cool and rich in water: we entered. For that matter it was not the first time we had accepted the hospitality of a woman, enchanted by the sight of Joseph. Only widows, who had no brothers-in-law at hand to marry them, could behave so freely. As a rule they were women no longer young, who displayed towards my master an explosion of love, part sinful and part maternal; often ugly, they would be bold one minute, shy and confused the next. Joseph treated them with courtesy and respect, flattering them just enough. And when he went off, he left behind a woman moved and pleased with herself, confident in the future.

The beauty of the village near Schechem led us to an arbour near an enormous fig tree. There was a table; the servants brought food.

Our hostess spoke little and smiled a great deal, as is proper in a polite woman. Her food was good, and the wine even better. She and my master, rising from the table, went for a stroll in the garden, and at a certain point they must have lain down in the grass because I saw them no more. I lay down under the fig tree and fell asleep.

We went away as the air was growing cool. At the gate there was a surprise in store for us: they had stolen the ass. My first thought was 'serves him right'; I was referring not to the ass, but to Joseph and his logical reasoning. To be sure, nobody steals a cask of nails (though this, too, is just possible), but there is more than one rogue ready to steal the ass which bears the cask. A moment later I sank again into that desperation that had overwhelmed me after the fake theft in the inn of Jerusalem. Seated in the dust, I refused to move.

Joseph was not totally a master: otherwise he would have kicked me. Instead, he started walking in the direction of the high road, and a little later, I followed him. The thief who had stolen the ass was not interested in carpenter's tools, or else was afraid that the heavy burden would slow down the animal he was escaping with: along our way he had scattered our entire supply of the tools of our craft. We found first the saw, the tool that takes up most room, then the planes, hammers, and chisels. A bit farther on we saw also the cask, spilled on to the road, nails scattered all around.

'He noticed the coins,' Joseph said, 'that were glittering in a different way from the nails,' and he stopped to pick them up. He didn't forget even one.' He walked on for a few cubits and announced to me, reading the tracks: 'Here he stopped again, perhaps to count them.' Deeper prints could be observed in the dust, the man's, as well as the marks left by the hoofs of the restless ass, overlapping one another.

'Here he set off again,' Joseph said. 'He wanted to run, but the ass held him back.' He bent to look at the streaks that the stubborn ass had left with his hoofs, resisting. 'Fool, why don't you leave the ass behind? What are you waiting for? With just one of those coins you can buy three or four asses.'

And, in fact, at a bend in the road, our animal came towards us, braying. Of all his burden only the packsaddle was left. We loaded the tools and the nails after making some fuss over the poor ass, who was in no way responsible for the theft; and we resumed our journey.

No, he was not responsible. But what about the widow who had called us from the wall? Joseph said we had no proof, and as far as he was concerned he did not even have any suspicions.

IV

The distance between Jerusalem and Nazareth can be covered in two days: it took us three, because we were downcast and full of hunger. We could have sold the ass, a big, handsome animal, pale grey in colour; but we didn't even give it a thought. For us by now he was a friend.

I have observed that the people of Israel make sacrifice to the Lord of many kinds of animal, but never asses; they are too fond of these companions in labour and travel. I must say I understand them.

We were taken in by a dumb peasant who lived in a hut not far from Nazareth, on a hill. We had arrived at the door of his house one evening, when it was already dark and had asked shelter. In these parts you roast during the day, and at night your teeth chatter. A little man opened the door, gesticulating, and invited us to the fire. The room, the one room of the house, stank like a stable, but to us it seemed a womb. Our host, dumb but not deaf, offered us fresh milk, cheese, and carobs. He owned a dozen sheep, which, a little later, were crowded into the same room with us.

'How can he live here?' Joseph murmured. 'It's stifling.' We went outside for a moment to renew our supply of air.

We stayed in that house a full day, studying the city, which lay over the hill opposite. Nazareth is a real city: not a town, like Bethlehem. It has almost a thousand inhabitants. Scattered over the slope, it is all white. Only about a dozen of the houses have two storeys; the others have at most one room on the flat roof, open as a rule, used to take the cool air in summer.

I don't know the reason why Joseph wanted to stay here, in Nazareth. I didn't like the idea. Perhaps I had come to share the prejudices I learned in Bethlehem about the Galileans.

They are ignorant peasants, who do not know the fine points of the Law or else care nothing for them. The rest of the people of Israel are in agreement: nothing good can come out of Galilee.

The dumb man acted as our guide in the discovery of Nazareth. The first person we came upon, a woman sweeping the dirt out of the door of her house, greeted him and called him by name; and so we learned that our new friend was called Nathan. Up at the hut there was no one to tell us. The woman withdrew immediately into the house, as if intimidated by the sight of two strangers; I could see her eyes at a chink, gazing greedily at Joseph. An area of repressed desires, in my opinion, the people there were rougher than in Bethlehem, their manners stern and rustic. Everything confirmed this view: there was nowhere a woman in sight; at the market only crones or maidservants. There was no sign of that interest in elegance that in Judaea made women's dress different, in tiny details: the way a kerchief was tied over the head, a ribbon in the hair, brightly coloured sandals and belts. Here the dominant colour was dark grey.

In all the territory of Israel wealth is badly distributed; a few lords, with lands, palaces, and slaves, a smattering of humble people, and then the poor. In Nazareth there was no one building that overpowered the others, like the palace of Herod in Jericho or that of the Asmonaeans in Jerusalem. We walked past larger, two-storey houses, built in the lower, central part of the city; the other dwellings were mean, one or two rooms, like Nathan's hovel, but scrupulously painted white and, it seemed, very clean.

A group of children was coming home from school, led by an old woman. They were frisking, leaping like goats to work off the restlessness accumulated on their benches, the boredom of having repeated for hours the same verses of the Law. They were all boys, naturally. Girls learn to recite the Law at home, from the mouths of the grown-ups, who thus go over the lesson themselves.

I was surprised to hear a little female voice, calling: 'Joseph! Joseph!' It was only when the troop of students had passed that we saw a little girl standing at the door of one of the larger houses. 'Joseph of Bethlehem,' she cried joyously and motioned us to come to her. Obviously they had warned her not to go away, or she would have come to us. It was her, all right, the little girl my master made the cart for, before we left: Maria. She was leaping up and down in her happiness and she flung her arms around Joseph's neck.

'You've come,' she murmured to him, pleased. 'You've come to Nazareth.' And she went on: 'You see where I live? Here, in this house, with my uncle and aunt.'

Nathan waved a greeting to Maria: the pair knew each other. They exchanged smiles. The child had great respect for the dumb man, because he could talk with his hands; he was someone extraordinary. Perhaps to her it seemed inevitable that the dumb man had encountered Joseph at once, because to her eyes my master was also an extraordinary man.

Joseph was pleased that the child remembered him. It seemed to him a sign, finding her again; it was an invitation to stay. He liked it when she took his hand, pestered him with all sorts of questions: how are you? why are you here? what are you doing? will you stay here always?

Joseph carefully answered them all; he knew that children are never given complete and satisfactory answers, and he tried to make sure that his would satisfy Maria's curiosity. At the last – 'will you stay here always?' – he stopped to think about this fundamental question, involving his future; and he sought her encouragement: 'What do you say?'

The little girl had no doubts: 'Oh, yes, stay. It's nice here. There's lots of honey. Today at my house there's ox tail for dinner. And there is plenty of wood: great big trees on the hills.'

'I'll stay,' Joseph promised. He did not say it lightly, with that condescension people use to keep children quiet. He had come to a decision. The child was not the cause or the reason for his intention to stay. She only contributed, he told her, to turning his wishes more in one direction than another.

Maria had another question: 'Do you still have my stone? The little one with the yellow streaks? I still have your cart; I play with it every day.'

'It brought me luck,' Joseph said, digging into his pocket.

'It wasn't supposed to bring you luck – only to make you remember me.'

'I remember you, don't I?' Joseph searched anxiously; he was embarrassed.

'You've lost it,' the girl remarked, desolate. Maria started to cry, unable to hold back the great tears that silently trickled down her cheeks.

'I'm sorry,' he murmured, contrite.

'You know why you lost it? Because you don't love me.' And she went back into the house, slamming the door.

We went back to Nathan's hut to sleep. The dumb man was very jolly and lively, always bustling about. In him, the necessity for expression became a teeming of the fingers, an endless series of gestures. His finger language was not alphabetic; it was a play of imagination and mime. It took some perception to understand it because Nathan would use one gesture but give it different meanings, according to the situation. If he made a pair of horns with his index and little fingers extended, he might mean an ox, or men (for him they were all cuckolds), a pitchfork, or the Romans. At times, the gesture became an exorcism. Many of his signs had to do with sheep: he would mime their milking, or pet their wool or move his fingers across the table to imitate their walk, prim and rapid. Joseph devoted much attention to him, and the little man quickly became fond of him.

After a couple of days, we held council. My master wanted to stay in Nazareth; I did not agree very wholeheartedly, but naturally I said yes. I would stay with him. What would we do? Probably we would be itinerant carpenters, the kind that walk around with a wood-shaving over one ear like a sign, going from house to house to repair cupboards, tables, chairs, divans, chests. Half-seriously, Joseph talked about a house he had seen for sale: two large ground floor rooms, and another on the roof, sheds and outbuildings in the yard. It was going cheap because the roof had to be redone: the rain, instead of running off, was soaking into the walls. The door was off its hinges. We could buy it and set up shop, I said, only if Simeon, the owner, were to give it to us for nothing.

Then, with a magician's wave of the hand, Joseph produced three gold coins, Greek-minted, undoubtedly from old Jacob's purse. He had hidden them in his tunic, he said, just in case of need.

The next day we went to Simeon. The smith accepted the three gold pieces as the first part of his payment. The rest would be paid in instalments, every six months.

Now Joseph was the owner. I was his employee, and so was Nathan, who would work with us a few hours each day as apprentice carpenter and handyman. Joseph was a born master: he spoke with his mild voice, but his words had the ring of orders. He was fond of me and Nathan, but he considered it natural for us to obey him.

We repainted the rooms as best we could and opened the shop, driving a stake in the ground at the gate in the courtyard wall, and hanging an old axe there as our sign. Tomorrow we would begin.

Our first customer turned up that same day, just before evening: it was Maria. She came into the yard and peered into the ground-floor room we used as workshop. We were still arranging it, with a new bench in the centre; we were hanging up tools, sweeping the sawdust. What I mean is, we didn't pay much attention to the child. We just greeted her and went on. Maria stayed there, by the door, in an attitude that must have had a special meaning for her: a bit stiff, a bit haughty, the attitude of a customer who feels neglected.

Finally Joseph realized the situation and went to take the order. Maria wanted a box, in which she could keep her valuables, not jewels but little things, each with its story: a little sack, for example, in which she was keeping her baby-teeth. She was clutching two drachmas in her fist; she wanted to leave them as a down-payment. Joseph refused them.

'You'll never get ahead in business, if you refuse your customers' money,' Maria said.

'Serious customers never pay in advance.'

This statement convinced her. She lingered a few more moments, to watch our work, smugly, as if the shop were also hers.

That evening we slept for the first time in the new house. Joseph made a bed for himself, not in the room next to where we worked, which served as pantry and kitchen, but in the upper room, on the roof; I created my own nest in one of the sheds in the yard. Nathan spent the nights in his house on the hill, with the sheep; he came down to work mid-morning and climbed back up again before sunset.

The dumb man understood the importance of raw material, and he would arrive with a beam on his back, a seasoned log, a vineyard stake. We never asked him where he got them.

Then Joseph discovered that it was Maria who told her friend where to find the pieces of wood. She had no idea it was wrong: she considered them abandoned, nobody's property, and, in fact, most of the pieces had been left at the back of a house or at the end of a yard.

'But it's the same as stealing,' Joseph said to her.

'No,' she said. 'Nobody uses them. They're just lying there, forgotten. And besides, if the owners don't come to ask for them back, it means they really did throw them away.' She was mistaken. Somebody did come wanting his goods back, and it was Elias, another carpenter who had had a shop in Nazareth for many years, our direct rival! Apparently Nathan had taken some wood also from his yard.

Elias's nickname, and here nicknames always had a reason, was 'Mortise'. It seemed that his great boast was that he never used nails, but joined the various parts of a piece of furniture only with mortises. But the name also had a second meaning, and referred to the carpenter's quarrelsome nature, his fondness of getting his adversaries into a tight corner.

Joseph welcomed him politely. He took him out to the yard to show him the wood we keep in a shed, so Elias could say if he recognized anything of his. My master was in good faith; he didn't know that, with Maria's complicity, Nathan had hidden the beams stolen from Mortise, hanging them down inside the well. Joseph asked permission of Elias to come to him for advice and instruction, soothing the cantankerous carpenter, who then went off, appeased. He was a man of temperament, not of character: it was all a question of knowing how to handle him.

Once his competitor had left, Joseph called us all together, including Maria, who appeared at the shop as often as she could and happened to be there at that moment, too. Had we all gone crazy? he asked us: did we want to get ourselves expelled from the city? Had we forgotten the commandment of Moses? He spoke very well, with the right amount of vehemence and sorrow. Maria was the one most affected by his speech: she burst into tears, and he had to console her. The child had acted with the best of intentions, and she did wrong only because she was so fond of him. Nathan knew what she was doing and considered it to be all right. As for me, I had always stolen trivial items but I had never lowered myself to the point of taking a piece of wood.

Soon it was no longer necessary to steal. We began to buy our logs on the nearby mountains, dressing them, putting them out in the open to season, and then in one of the sheds in the yard. Most of our work was crude stuff: the local farmers would bring us their wagons to mend or would order a yoke from us. Little jobs they did for themselves: they replaced the handle of the spade and the pitchfork, they all knew how to carve spoons for the house from pieces of wood. The inhabitants of the city, at least the ones who didn't go out to work in the fields, brought us broken chairs, bread bins, or called us to plane doors which had swollen with the dampness and wouldn't close properly.

I was assigned to do the cooking. I cooked only once a day, usually outdoors, under the portico. Over an open fire in a hole between two stones I would slowly cook a soup of broad beans or of lentils, or I would roast a couple of fish on the coals. An old neighbour woman ground corn for us and took the flour to the oven. Nathan filtered and poured the wine. Each had his task, so little time was wasted, and we could get back to work promptly. Joseph sometimes prepared a special dish for us, a leg of lamb, or of kid, or else, after drying a handful of locusts in the sun, he would discard the heads and legs, pound them to a powder in a mortar and, adding honey and flour, make some cakes.

We worked hard, especially the first months (we had to pay the second instalment on the house) and the city accepted us as good and honest craftsmen. Joseph was welcome in the synagogue, the only public place he frequented. I am not a child of Israel, and to the synagogue I prefer the tavern.

Maria was our customer and our witness, friend and regular visitor, honorary partner in our league of carpenters and official admirer of my master Joseph. At eighteen, Joseph was at the age when, according to the holy scriptures of the children of Israel, a man was supposed to marry; and Maria, at the age of eight, would soon be emerging from childhood. Here girls marry even at thirteen or fourteen, turning from children into women quite suddenly. Until they are nine or ten, they are left free, protected by their innocence; immediately afterwards, they are charged with awareness, kept at home, not allowed to go out unless they are accompanied.

For a little longer Maria would be a carefree child, but she was looking towards the future with a ravenous eagerness. She helped her aunt at home, repeated the verses of the Law, played with other little girls, but she had a good deal of free time and she generally spent it with us. She would arrive here in the afternoon, cross the yard, peer in at the door. Joseph would nod, and then she entered.

As a rule she would install herself on a little stool, specially made for her. Joseph didn't want her roaming around, as she would have preferred. He was afraid she might hurt herself: there were too many sharp tools scattered along the bench or set on the floor. When she felt like it, Maria was allowed to smooth or polish, using wooden files and old woollen cloths dipped in oil. But she was rarely in a working mood. Her chief activity consisted of watching Joseph: what he did was unceasingly wondrous, whether he was driving a nail or stripping an old bough. She followed him with her eyes so intensely that her attention became dramatic, as if she were awaiting a miraculous event, as if Joseph might sprout wings or rise to the ceiling with no need for wings, by levitation.

These contemplative moments tired her: after a while Maria became distracted, Nathan would make faces at her, and the two would start laughing, or they would talk with their fingers, plotting some joke. Only the child could express herself with the mute in his language, because she was the only one who had learned it. It was a sight to see, the two of them waving their hands and arms very fast, intent, interrupting each other only to laugh.

I was always the victim: neither Maria nor Nathan would ever think of playing a joke on Joseph. I would glimpse a fine gold coin in the sawdust, where it had fallen no doubt from a customer's pouch. I didn't pick it up at once; I am not fond of underlining my moments of luck. I would wait until the end of the afternoon, when all had left, one this way, one that, and only then would I bend over to pick it up. Nothing doing. The coin stuck tenaciously to the packed earth, which is the flooring of our workshop. Light laughter would bubble up from behind the planks propped in one corner: Maria, with the help of Nathan and some carpenter's glue had devised the trick and foiled my greed.

Glue figured in numerous jokes: my hands would pick up

shavings, finding them unexpectedly sticky; a piece of my tunic would remain on the bench where I sat and from which I could not rise. I had to be careful of my every action because I never knew what the irrepressible child, with her faithful squire, had thought up. I brought down the hammer to drive a nail and the head of the hammer flew across the room. They took the saw apart and put it back together with the teeth facing the other way, so that I would work with satisfaction at the power of my arm, not realizing that I was not sawing the plank, but only tickling it.

But then I found a way to get back at them. I discovered the pair of them as they were slipping a wineskin filled with water into the hollow of an old log that I was to chop up to make some laths. They were already anticipating my amazement, my alarm, when at the stroke of my axe, the dead tree would spatter water everywhere. I removed the water and replaced it with another skin full of wine, Nathan's property naturally. As if by chance, at the moment when I set to work with the axe the next day, there they were, the two of them. I brought down the blow, keeping my distance, and Maria was struck by a spurt that got her all wet; Nathan understood the trick and groaned in despair at the loss of his wine. That time I was the one who laughed.

Joseph waited until Maria sat beside him as he worked, for a little private conversation, and he scolded her. She was always happy to chatter for a moment with my master: that was the climax of the whole afternoon. Maria blushed with pleasure because Joseph talked to her as he would to an adult.

Joseph had never had to reproach her before. The child was not used to scoldings and she reacted furiously.

'I didn't do anything wrong. I was just joking.'

'Yes, but you've played a lot of jokes, and *always* on the same person.'

'I knew it,' she replied, 'Socrates has come to you and complained. He has no sense of humour.'

Joseph produced all his best arguments to prove to her that she was wrong: I had not appealed to him, and even if I had, it would be the same thing. A joke is forgivable if it does no harm, true; but the humiliation it inflicts on the victim is also harmful; and so on. Maria would not let herself be convinced.

'You're an old man!' she shouted at Joseph and ran off,

herself frightened by an epithet that must have seemed to her an insult and an accusation.

Their disagreement resembled a lovers' quarrel, between two people who are beginning to know each other and are discovering that fondness does not soften character. Maria reappeared at the shop three days later. Gravely, she came straight to Joseph and asked: 'Do you want me to ask your forgiveness?'

Joseph replied, with dignity: 'That's not necessary.'

'All right then,' Maria concluded and after a while managed to behave as usual, as if nothing had happened. But she played no more tricks on me.

Obviously there was no harm in the fact that an eight-year-old girl spent a part of her day in a shop with three men, but Joseph felt it would be a good idea to make the acquaintance of her uncle and aunt. Maria prepared the visit, and showed him into the house when he knocked on the door. It was a large house, about ten rooms built around a central court, and the same number on the upper floor, with a loggia that ran around all four sides of the court. With the child leading him, Joseph climbed some stone stairs and, after crossing a part of the loggia, he entered one of the rooms where the master and mistress of the house awaited him.

A cushion had been placed on a stool and there, majestically, sat Cleophas, Maria's uncle, the son of Jair. He was one of the three judges of the Tribunal of Nazareth: his post explained his solemnity and suggested his wealth, because as everyone knows, judges receive no payment. Both in body and in spirit he resembled the archetype of the perfect judge, as the books describe him: large, dignified, a linguist (and therefore requiring no interpreters, who are slipshod and corruptible), neither too young nor too old, expert in the magic arts, so as not to be deceived by tricks and witchcraft.

In one respect Cleophas did not correspond to the ideal judge: he was a pompous gossip. He was called Synedrion because several times he had been on the point of election to that august body, which is not only a tribunal for serious crimes against religion, but also a political and theological council. The enlightenment that Cleophas could bring to the Synedrion in matters of politics and theology, which here are practically the same thing, is beyond my understanding.

Joseph faced him as if he were one of life's little irritations: at times rain falls from the sky, and Maria had an uncle like this. Cleophas discoursed to him for five minutes on the political conditions of Israel and the need for stricter observance of the law of the Sabbath repose; he made a passing reference to Maria ('a bright child but too lively'), then dismissed the visitor. In Joseph's view, the judge had done nothing but wonder what was the precise motive of this young man's coming; and the older man heaved a sigh of relief when the youth left, having asked no favour of him and presented no petition.

Cleophas's wife was as curious as her husband, or perhaps even more; she held the visitor in the loggia, talking about her sister Elizabeth, who lived near his city, Bethlehem. Unobtrusively, she was inquiring about Joseph's family, using the familiar pretext of looking for relatives in common. There were some, and so she was convinced that my master's background was respectable.

She had liked Joseph immediately. At supper that evening she happened to say, speaking with her husband and telling him how Joseph came from a good family, that, at the age of twenty, David must have looked like him. The judge huffed impatiently and said that, when still a boy, David held first a slingshot, then a sword in his hand, whereas Joseph's weapon, or so it seemed, was a plane. Furthermore, a man that handsome, he said, made him uneasy and impelled him to treat the other like a woman.

'Badly, in other words,' his wife murmured, in a low voice, but not so low that Cleophas could not hear her.

'I hope he doesn't resemble David in another way. Be careful. You entrust Maria to him so calmly. Take care, when the child is a little older.'

The woman did not understand, and Cleophas did not condescend to enlighten her. The maidservant later took the trouble to remind her mistress how the great king loved to conquer both cities and women.

V

Joseph had realized at once that in Nazareth there would be no way for him to resume the game with girls as in Bethlehem. Young women came out rarely and then always accompanied; the well was not a special, popular place as in droughtridden Judaea. Here many families had water in the court of their house, a well or a brook, and in the streets you often saw drinking-troughs for animals and washing-places for clothes. At synagogue gatherings the families came in a body, and fathers and mothers kept an eye on the veiled heads of their daughters.

But where there is a prohibition, a way around it is always found. Some of the young men allowed themselves to be seduced by a girl's graces, and arranged secret meetings with her, usually in the garden of her house. As everyone knew, the matter could end only in marriage: if the parents did not become aware of the trysts on their own, the girl would take care that they were informed so that she could be caught by surprise.

A unanimous cry, or rather a whisper, summed up the young males' point of view on this situation: 'Never girls from your home town.' But then, when they ventured into the nearby towns, they encountered the same situation: abstinence or marriage. And in the end they made love with prostitutes.

We were beginning to earn real money; Joseph went into debt and bought himself a horse. Horses are rare in Israel, and are considered a sign of luxury and arrogance. My master's was used to reach the cities that were a bit more distant, where perhaps the women were less shy. It offered a way of getting out of Nazareth, in other words, where too many marriageable girls were plotting to get a husband.

Joseph felt pursued, dogged; he couldn't take a step without a pair of black eyes spying on him from behind some shutters. In the Ropemakers' street, where nubile girls are more numerous, sighs followed him from one house to the next and could be heard distinctly in the street. And the young wives joined the maidens, not because they actually thought of betraying their husbands (which was practically impossible, as the women lived in segregation under the watchful guard of mothers-in-law and sisters-in-law), but simply for the pleasure of tormenting themselves with an unhappy love.

One of the prettiest girls one day managed to draw him into the inner rooms of her house, assuring him that no one was at home. He believed her: Iona, daughter of Judas, was irresistible in her tunic with its embroidered hem; her eyes were tender; she smiled freely, and was only thirteen. Joseph had no thought of doing anything compromising: at most he would have kissed her: an action that leaves no stain. In the shadowy room he bent down to pick up the silk fillet that had slipped from his head: from beneath the curtains he saw the feet of a man and a woman protruding; and without even straightening his back, he left the way he had come. The girl ran after him to the door of the house, calling 'Joseph! Joseph!', but my master was already around the corner.

After he had bought the horse, it was much more difficult to catch Joseph off guard. Once or twice a week he would climb into the saddle at dawn, when the sky was beginning to brighten, and he would come back at night. More often he went out at sunset and took a ride until supper time. The only other horses in the city were beasts of burden, and nobody could chase him to see where he was going.

The adult population of Nazareth was in agreement, criticizing my master's conduct. They considered him presumptuous and spendthrift, predicting that his vanity would be the ruin of him. The girls, on the contrary, peeped from behind the shutters and found something regal about Joseph, as he swayed on the horse; and they dreamed that he would hoist them into the saddle in front of him and carry them off for a ride like that, in glory.

Only Maria enjoyed this privilege. Joseph would hand her the reins and, with his arms around her to prevent her falling, he would urge Saul to a trot, through the streets of Nazareth. Maria had the impression that she was directing the horse, regulating his pace all by herself; and she would swell with proud happiness. She would remember it all her life. She told me, years later, that there had never been a more triumphant moment for her than those rides, when she would close her eyes and Joseph would mingle with Saul, man and horse becoming a single, magic creature.

Saul was a Berber horse, imported from Africa, long, medium-weight, an excellent saddle-horse. In the taverns of Nazareth and at the inn they talked about him for months: there were lively arguments about his maximum speed, his staying power, the amount of special oats he consumed, especially on the days when he had to race. The best-informed ventured hypotheses about the price he might have cost. In a word, the men and the boys envied my master.

Then when they calculated all the places (distant and foreign for them, who went on foot or, at most, mounted an ass) that could be reached with such a horse in a single morning, they were consumed by the thought that such luck should have befallen a foreigner, and a Judaean at that. Joseph paid no attention. At eighteen, he was at the glorious peak of adolescence, and any active release was a delight for him: running, riding, working, loving. He had no time to pay attention, to worry; but I had the time and the age, and I was concerned for him. To spark, in the space of a few months, the desire of all the women and the envy of all the men can be dangerous.

I soon found out that Joseph's preferred destination on his one-day outings was Ptolemais, a half-Greek city on the coast. He would go there the day before the Sabbath, so on his return he could rest. The Law imposes such overwhelming inactivity on the day consecrated to the Lord that, as Joseph said, if you didn't wear yourself out the day before, you wouldn't be able to put up with an entire day of idleness. When the trumpet sounded three times at nightfall through the whole following Sabbath day, life came to a stop. It was forbidden to light a fire or to walk more than six stadia, to tie or untie a knot, to write more than one letter of the alphabet. All you could do was pray.

Joseph prayed conscientiously and then he writhed on his bed in the upper room, recalling in his memory the sensations enjoyed in Ptolemais. It was beautiful to ride through the morning in the plain of Esdraelon with, on your left, the long, bony outline of the hills of Carmel, and before you and around you the fertile countryside, lush and green. And, emerging from those pastoral surroundings, from the profound quiet that accompanied the wayfarer for long stretches of his journey, you reached a lively and industrious city, with a varicoloured populace, with always-different human encounters.

After leaving his horse stabled on the outskirts of the city, Joseph went at an easy pace as far as the harbour, alert to the spectacle continually offered in the streets by the passersby themselves: Phoenicians wearing embroidered trousers under their tunics; Syrian merchants swathed in silks; men with goatskin cloaks coming from the plains of Anatolia; sailors from the islands, an apron tight around their waists and a strip of canvas tied around their hair. The women were a spectacle apart, as they mixed in the male throng without embarrassment or fear: the little Nubian servant-girl dressed in yellow and red, her white teeth gleaming in contrast with her black skin; the elegant prostitute, who proceeded with her head veiled but with her breasts almost totally bared; and the rich lady hastening towards her litter, accompanied by a handmaiden. Some ladies, to indicate their position as married women, denied the approach of any man other than their husband, wore a short golden chain linking their ankles, and they walked in tiny steps: Joseph found them very exciting for this reason alone.

The miraculous thing was that the women of Ptolemais could be freely addressed, and no one made any objection; even unmarried girls would answer in a straightforward tone and go along with a jest. Joseph struck up conversation with all of them, enchanted by the very nearness of a female form, by the fleeting intimacy established between him and them through the exchange of a smile or a word. He went from one to another, along the street, at the market, the washing-place. Not because he tired of the one who was near but because he was reluctant to miss out on those farther off: he wanted to be with them all, to speak with two or three at a time. He swam in femininity, in a laughing and sweet-smelling sea.

It was not difficult to go further, to accept one of the many invitations, some even quite explicit, that were addressed to him; and that is what Joseph did.

The moment was approaching when Simeon had to be paid

another instalment on the house he had sold us, and we didn't have even half of the necessary sum. Our earnings were theoretically much greater, but we were forced to extend credit to our customers who paid their bills when they felt like it.

After sunset Joseph walked with Maria to her house if she had stayed longer than usual, and he would take her by the hand because the child was afraid of the looming darkness. One evening he heard her ask: 'Where will you find the money, Joseph?'

He was irked that one of us, perhaps Nathan, perhaps me, had hinted to the child of our troubles, but he was flattered that she took his business affairs so much to heart.

'If necessary, I'll sell my horse.'

'No, please, don't do that,' Maria begged, and she tugged at his arm. 'That would be a crime,' she concluded, using an expression she had picked up from the conversation of the grown-ups.

The next day she handed over her savings to him, a few drachmas and a number of little copper coins. Joseph, who understood children, did not mortify her with a refusal: he vowed to repay the money within a month, with interest. Maria felt more and more involved in our firm's fortunes, and she looked around the shop with a proprietary dignity, so much so that she was a bit disappointed on being demoted back to her role as regular visitor when my master returned the little sum, along with the agreed interest.

When I think back and see again our little band then, I realize that it must have seemed violently unusual to an outsider: a young man as handsome as a Greek god; a reddish wall-eyed man (this was me); a mute; a little girl.

When we had only two days left before our payment fell due, a peasant from Bethlehem came in, a man Joseph knew because he worked in the house of Joseph's father. He brought a little bag of coins. They were not that many and not all were of gold but they were more than enough to extricate us from our difficulties. In a separate little bag Joseph found the signet ring that Jacob always wore on his finger, and then he fell to weeping – his old father was dead. His father had sent him the money, a farewell present, but also the ring which meant that in spirit his father considered him his first-born, the son who would continue the line.

For three days my master refused to speak or work; and he observed mourning for a month. Maria, who saw him dirty and bearded, for he did not shave or wash in all this period, respected his grief and rarely spoke to him.

One day I heard them talking quietly, seated on the doorstep of the shop, facing the yard. It was the sunset hour. Nathan had gone back up to his hut. They thought they were alone. I had entered the shop, behind them, from the rear door, not wanting to disturb them by making my presence known.

'Your father has joined his fathers, up in heaven, hasn't he?' Maria asked. 'He was a just man and now he will receive his reward.'

Joseph nodded; she was right.

'Then,' Maria continued, 'why are you crying?'

'I'm crying for myself, not for him. I never loved him enough while he was alive; I brought sorrow to his old age.' Joseph accused himself of having been an egoist. 'We become generous,' he said, 'when it's too late.'

Seated beside him, Maria put her hand on his shoulder, in one of those adult gestures that now and then came to her spontaneously. The sun had set and the breeze was coming down from the mountains, heralding the cold of the night. Joseph stood up: 'I'll see you home,' he said.

Maria also stood up. 'I will have no regrets,' she said. 'I will always be generous with you. I'll love you as myself.'

Joseph looked at her in amazement. He said no more. He took her by the hand, and they went off across the yard.

Uncle Cleophas disapproved of Maria's association with us carpenters, folk of low degree who knew the Law only in a summary, helter-skelter fashion and attended the synagogue as seldom as possible, namely only for Sabbath prayer. With the excuse that a judge must know well the people that represent his official concern, Synedrion had developed his curiosity; originally no more than an ordinary fault, it had become a demanding passion.

He asked a number of questions about us: how we managed to get along, how my master had been able to pay Simeon on the due date, what his niece found in us, why Joseph was so good-looking. This final question was more a complaint raised to the author of all things, who gave beauty to a young, thoughtless Judaean and denied it to a deserving man. Cleophas was ugly – incomplete even in his flaws, you might say: he was not totally bald, but only halfway; his beard grew in clumps on his chin and he stubbornly did not shave it. Seated, he had an impressive appearance, but the moment he stood up you saw how short his legs were.

I believe he wanted to separate Maria from her carpenter chiefly out of jealousy, because the child loved the young man and to her uncle she dedicated only an absent and dutiful affection; because Joseph was young and women ran after him, whereas Cleophas had to limit himself to deploring the young women of today when he took the floor in the synagogue. He grumbled, at table, against young men who lack the money to pay their debts and yet ride around on a horse; he told stories about the treacherous nature of the Judaeans; in other words, he wanted his opposition to Joseph, fearful and grouchy as it was, to be clear to the women of the house. Prohibiting Maria to visit the carpenter was an idea that came to Cleophas's mind at least twice a day, when the child went out in the afternoon to go up to that 'wood-sawer', as he called Joseph, and when she came back. But he calculated the risk, and did not dare run it.

He would have been obeyed, of course, but he knew he was in the minority: his wife and his niece would have made him pay for his act of authority with little, incessant retaliations, and the child was no less fearsome than the adult. Cleophas gave up the idea. Still he did not lose the hope of discovering something about my master that would diminish him in Maria's eyes and in those of the community.

I realized immediately that he was spying on us. He would arrive late at night and look over the little wall, which came up to his shoulders; he would make a mental note if a light was still burning, or a pile of planks had been shifted; he would wonder if we received someone in secret, our accomplice in heaven knows what intrigues. At our place, especially at night, nothing ever happened; disappointed but not discouraged, Cleophas began to climb over the wall and venture into the yard. Who knows? Perhaps he thought to find something compromising hidden inside the sheds.

I warned Joseph, who smiled and told me not to disturb Cleophas, to let him spy as much as he liked. I am sorry to have to admit that, for once, I disobeyed.

In the yard, around the chicken house, we kept some wooden traps, jaws bristled with serrations, to protect us from the foxes, from the hills above the city. There was also a tub, in which, one night, we had prepared a cinnabar solution to paint a new cart the next morning. I didn't do *much*: I shifted the tub under the wall and placed a couple of traps nearby. An artisan has a right to put his belongings where he chooses in his own yard.

From behind the shed I kept watch and I had a moment of dejection: Synedrion had come, but he was hesitating to scale the wall: perhaps he sensed the danger. In the end he made up his mind: he stuck one leg over, he pulled up the other, and sat down. Then, with a little jump, he landed in the red paint, spattering it all the way up to his eyes. After a brief exclamation, like a hiccup, he was quiet. He was concerned about making noise, but he could not contain a scream, when he felt his ankle held fast in the fox trap.

Joseph lit a lantern and came down to see. Cleophas had not waited for him. Taking care especially not to be recognized, he had gone off, dragging his leg and carrying in his hand the stone that anchored the trap. If anyone had seen him, coloured a bright red, clambering along in that way, Synedrion would have lost his dignity forever, he would not be able to hold office as a judge any longer, and he would never have dared open his mouth again at a meeting in the synagogue.

The next day Maria came with the news that her uncle was in bed, ill. Cleophas had not been able to hide his wretched state from his wife, the paint and the trap. He had blamed the mishap on mysterious political enemies, stern Pharisees or Sadduccee separatists, (two sects that in Nazareth, however, had no followers). The woman had to believe that some people had come a long way to paint Judge Cleophas red, and to her this seemed a confirmation of her husband's importance.

From that time on Maria's uncle harboured a raging dislike of Joseph who had absolutely no responsibility for the jokes played on the judge. Speaking with his niece, he would refer to 'that good-for-nothing friend of yours', and with his wife he used even worse names, suited only to adult ears.

At that time Joseph really was not killing himself with his work. To begin with, he took a day off every week, in addition to the Sabbath, and then he left the hardest jobs to me and

Nathan. We dealt with the plough, the yokes, the wagons; he concerned himself with buckets, dippers, cutting-boards. Secretly I called him a ladies' carpenter. But, on the contrary, he was destined to achieve the dream of every craftsman: that of inventing a new and useful object, leaving his mark.

A number of women came to the shop, servant-girls or young married women, to order a stool or a big spoon, a coffer or a chair; and all of them invariably addressed Joseph, ignoring me and Nathan. Little, refined jobs, which demanded patience and care, amused Joseph. He would turn and file and polish; he would stroke the object produced by his hands as if it too were enlivened by the fascination of the customers who, though rather plain and drab, were still women and young. To his eyes they were all attractive, but he took care not to give them any encouragement.

Joseph was forced to maintain an even greater reserve because of his reputation as a womanizer; a young man who rode a racing horse like his already gave off a perfume of sin. You would have said that the greasy, clumsy maids who came to the shop could actually smell that perfume: even ordering a soup ladle from Joseph became an adventure. The thrill of remaining for a minute at his side, smelling in his hair the scent of guilty loves, of distant and sinful cities, was a way of taking part in his pleasures, of feeling loved and beautiful.

The ladies of Nazareth, about twenty married and well-to-do women, no longer sent for him to do jobs at home because they had learned by experience that he would send me or Nathan. Joseph did not want any trouble with married women.

The rumours of his successes with the women of Ptolemais, exaggerated as is the rule in these cases, had even reached Maria. Nor had the child failed to notice how frequently the Nazareth maidservants came to the shop to talk to him, with the excuse of giving him more precise instructions about the work they had ordered from him. By now Maria was nine and was about to discover many aspects of life that until then had been hidden from her. She had remarked, for example, that the female visitors did not like to speak to Joseph in her presence and would call him aside. This behaviour made her curious and she asked my master the reason why women wanted to be alone with him.

'I can't imagine,' he answered, embarrassed.

'Let's make it a game. We'll try to guess. What do you say it is?'

'They're afraid of you,' Joseph ventured, hoping to evade the issue.

'No,' Maria said proudly, 'they're jealous.'

Joseph pretended not to know that word and asked her what it meant.

'They're mad because I can be with you as much as I like, and they can't.'

'Is that all?' I said, joining in; between me and the child there were constant verbal jabs.

'No,' Maria replied, 'they would like to kiss Joseph like this,' and she gave him a resounding kiss on the cheek. 'I can, and they can't; they're too old for kissing.' Only Nathan burst out laughing, but it was true: our customers were too old for such childish displays of affection. And Maria was too young for kisses of another kind.

The next year she was able to understand a bit more. A girl who proved pregnant, also called Maria, daughter of Daniel, accused Joseph of having seduced her. Daniel's Maria was fifteen and was very beautiful; it is likely that the man really responsible was not acceptable as a husband or was not in a position to marry her: so, in league with her mother who was widowed by then, this Maria thought to trap my master.

The question could not be judged in the tribunal for lack of witnesses, but Cleophas was involved anyway because he was on the council of elders which met in the synagogue, behind closed doors to hear the two parties. It would have required a Solomon to decide who was telling the truth between the girl who accused and Joseph who denied.

My master was asked if he knew the plaintiff. Joseph replied that he had seen her once in his life. Asked to explain the circumstances of that meeting, he said: 'I saw a young woman walking ahead of me, shaking her whole person and shifting the weight of her body from one foot to the other. I asked the man with me if she was lame, and he answered that she walked like that to attract the attention of the passersby.'

The girl's mother emitted a cry of protest, especially since the grave members of the council had burst out laughing. The elders, however, did not know how to resolve the case: if Maria was considered frivolous and easy, Joseph's reputation suggested him as the likely one responsible for what happened. According to his accuser the outrage had taken place in the carpenter's yard, in broad daylight, among the bushes that grew between the sheds.

One of the elders recalled the chaste Susanna and her accusers who described the same tree, one as a terebinth, the other as a sycamore; and he asked what sort of bushes these were. After consultation with her mother, the sly Maria of Daniel said that she had paid no attention: they were just bushes, thick, short plants, very green.

'May I ask a question?'

Joseph was allowed to speak: 'Ask my accuser what colour the mark on my chest is.'

The women, mother and daughter, whispered for a moment, convinced that a trap was being set for them. Then Maria replied triumphantly: 'Joseph has no mark. His skin is everywhere smooth and white.'

At that point my master stood up, suddenly opened his tunic without asking anyone's permission and, devil take him, (it was a shock also for me, present there as witness): on his chest, under his right nipple, there was a wine-colored birthmark the size of a hand.

Taken aback, the two women looked at each other. 'I didn't know,' Maria said distinctly.

She was reprimanded and sentenced to pay a considerable fine, which Joseph turned over to the council itself for the relief of the poor.

When we were home again, Joseph showed me how easy it was simply to wash the birthmark away. I congratulated him on his trick.

'The innocent are in a bad way,' he said, laughing, 'if they're not smarter than the guilty.'

Maria, our Maria, wanted him to tell her exactly what it was he had been accused of. 'What did she say you did, and what do you have to do with it if she's going to have a baby?'

Joseph answered evasively, and Maria was not satisfied with his explanations. He asked her to go to her uncle Cleophas, who was the judge, after all, and knew more about it.

'I see,' Maria concluded sagely, having little intimacy with her uncle. 'I have to grow up.'

VI

Maria came into the yard and looked through the window, standing on tiptoe. We all knew she was there; we had heard the crunch of her sandals on the gravel, but we acted as if nothing had happened. At times we left her there for a long while, until she herself grew tired and revealed her presence by greeting us. Sometimes Joseph went out, going into the other room and, from there, into the yard; he would come around the house, stand behind her, and clap his hands over her eyes.

'You're Joseph!' she would cry, with her little piping voice.

One afternoon I also put my hands over her eyes. I was coming from the shed and she had not yet seen me, but through the window she could clearly see Joseph working at the bench. 'You're Joseph!' she cried, I cannot say why. I felt a twinge of envy of my master, whom she must consider ubiquitous if he could be bent over his work in the shop and, at the same time, in the yard, covering her eyes with his hands.

For some time, as she was growing older, Maria had been staying less and less with us, as if she herself realized it was not right for a young girl, now grown, to spend so much time with men. I looked at her when she went off, her shawl wrapped tightly around her as if she were a little woman. She no longer hopped and skipped, or ran as she used to; now she imitated the sedate walk of the women here, their eyes lowered. But she raised her feet too high and her little wooden clogs struck the stones merrily

Joseph didn't think to make her a pair carved from an olive branch; Nathan did that, nailing to the wood a strip of fine red leather. When the dumb man gave them to her, Maria burst into tears. Nathan didn't understand her reaction. But I did: Maria would have wanted the clogs to come from Joseph.

The girl made her visits less frequent. She came back to greet us in the shop two or three times in the space of a month, then she came no more. We realized that she had received her revelation. Her aunt had explained everything to her; the animal part of human relations, but also the consolatory part, the feelings that enhance them. And finally, still mysterious for Maria, the pleasure promised to women and not always achieved that is sought by instinct, often feared as something guilty and always paid for with suffering: life with a man, motherhood.

At ten Maria now knew what a woman knows, but she remained innocent. She considered Joseph with indulgence, like an older sister, and with a new awe: for her he had suddenly become a man and she could not look at him without shyness, and this made him embarrassed too. Something burdensome had come between them, an awareness that extinguished the laughter and the jokes. Every word, every act now had to be measured and weighed; they could no longer be light-hearted and spontaneous as in the past. Maria was enclosed in a new world and she had to learn how to move; she was taller and heavier, a woman and not a child.

Joseph no longer went to Ptolemais so frequently but only when the boredom of Nazareth overcame him. One day, tired of the same teeming humanity that at first had so attracted him, he spent almost all his time at the harbour, looking at the sea. He retraced his way across the city towards evening. At the stables his horse was gone, or rather they swore they had already given it back to him. Protests, reasoning, pleas were of no avail. Joseph realized that someone, with the complicity of the stable-boys, had stolen his horse, which by now was surely far away God knows where.

When my master threatened to turn to Herod's soldiers and have them arrested, the men of the stables surrounded him and struck him with their searing whips. Then they hid him, half-unconscious, in the straw of the yard.

Joseph came to when it was dark, dragged himself to the well, drank, washed, then prepared to return home on foot. It took him the whole night.

It was thus that he lost his horse and his self-confidence.

I had risen at dawn and was drawing up a bucket of water

from the well to wash my face when I saw, looking over the wall, a form I seemed to recognize. The man was limping and advancing with great effort, exhausted. It was Joseph. I went to him, carrying a cloak. I led him into the house and, after building a fire, I put a cauldron of water to heat. When he had washed and eaten something, my master's teeth stopped chattering, and he slept until evening.

Joseph remained shut up in the house, tending his wounds and his dejection. At evening he came down to the yard and sat among the piles of logs.

'How have I spent my life so far?' he said to me one night. 'Looking and being looked at. What relations have I had with my fellow-man? My fellow-man is all women . . .'

I don't know what thoughts had gone through his head during that long night of his return from Ptolemais, but Joseph was no longer light-hearted as he had been until just a short time before. He was maturing, and he didn't like it. Now the excursions to Ptolemais were out of the question. We were making good money, but the purchase of another horse was inconceivable. Joseph was still paying for the one stolen from him. He felt trapped again, tied to Nazareth, where sex meant marriage.

All the same he began to take an interest in the girls of the city, whom he had neglected until then. Not in the daytime, not openly, but at night-fall and in secret. He had only to sit in the shadow below the wall of a house and hear the women's voices as they were going to bed, the girls joking, the soft cadence of their laughter muffled by sleepiness. At times he could also make out the words, when the window was not high from the ground and stood open; in those cases he could also see the shadows of the girls as they undressed, cast by the lamp against the wall of the house opposite.

Monotony and boredom do nothing but lengthen our days: years roll by, one after another, and we are amazed that they have passed. Joseph measured how much uneventful time had gone by without his notice, then one day he had a surprise.

He had learned to follow girls in the street. He would choose those who were escorted, by a maid or by an elderly woman relative; and feel safer! The escort chiefly protected him, restrained him, prevented him from doing anything foolish, like speaking directly to the girl or allowing himself to be seen in her company. He would walk at a distance of ten paces, not so close as to seem indiscreet, nor so far as to be unable to appreciate, with a connoisseur's eye, the sway of the hips, the ankles peeping from beneath the skirt, the slender neck, the erect carriage of the head.

One afternoon, when he was going to pay the man who hired out wagons, he saw from behind a girl turning into a side street. He hesitated barely a moment, then chose to forget he was going in a different direction, and followed her. Tall and lithe, the beauty (for such she must have been, to judge from the other side) walked along with an old woman humbly dressed in black, a servant or perhaps her old nurse. Joseph was sure the girl was newly-arrived in the town, otherwise he could not have failed to notice her before. He watched the tender heels that rose and fell in their sandals, the slim ankles, the beginning of the calves and, above, the waist girded by a belt, the straight shoulders, the head covered by a shawl. The strange girl emanated seductiveness as a flower gives off its scent: she did nothing, that is, to attract attention, but Joseph could not take his eyes off her. He realized, in a confused way, that this girl was different from those he had known before.

Then something happened that made him think 'this one, too, is like the others.' She dropped a little piece of cloth on the ground. Joseph, who had often avoided picking up things that girls sowed along their path to attempt an approach of some kind, could not resist this time. He picked up the object, which was a little cloth case, a purse, and ran after the woman to return it.

The girl turned at his call and smiled at him, as if at an old friend, cordially in other words and without any slyness. It was a moment before he recognized her: it was Maria, and she was very beautiful.

'It's mine,' the old woman said. 'Thank you, sir; you are kind.'

Joseph held out the purse and bowed.

'I thank you, too, Joseph,' Maria added, and said goodbye to him, 'The Lord be with you.' She turned her back and resumed her way.

My master realized he had not said a word; he also realized

that she was very pleased at having aroused such obvious admiration in him. How was it possible that the little girl had grown so? A year before, or two years, say, she had been little more than a child, tall and skinny, her shoulder-blades protruding. Joseph had had few occasions to see her lately and she in the meanwhile had become like this. Like this? How? Grown up, he said to himself, and he added nothing else, not even mentally, because in placing her alongside the beautiful women he had known, in thinking of her physical attributes, her body, in other words, it seemed to him that he was showing her disrespect.

This encounter left him uneasy. Joseph suffered because his paternal fondness for Maria no longer existed, and he would not concede that it had become desire. A sense of hostility and, at the same time, awe had arrested him before her, as if she was suddenly alien and fearful.

VII

Joseph stopped talking about women. I became alarmed because until then it had been his favourite subject, an endless theme. There was nothing memorable about his ideas on the opposite sex, unless you count the reasons he brought up to justify his preference for widows and in particular for those who had no children or other relatives.

'You mustn't think I only want to avoid risks and responsibility,' he used to say to me. 'I'm also concerned not to cause the woman any harm. You know the disadvantages they have, compared to us men, here in my country.'

I did know: watched, locked up, stoned if found in adultery, forced to marry a brother-in-law if left widows and without resources, the women of Israel do not have a happy life but toil, sacrifice, and religion. When they reach a certain age, they often turn shrewish or become tireless gossips. You have no idea how much a woman can chatter, unless you have come within range of certain women of Galilee. They seem to release in words what they are not allowed to translate into actions. As the rabbi said: 'The Lord gave the human race ten bags of words, and women took nine of them . . . '

According to Joseph, in relations with the female sex you must try not to wrong anyone. How does the commandment go? 'Thou shalt not covet thy neighbour's wife.'

Now a widow belongs only to herself. But what about that other commandment: 'Thou shalt not commit impure acts?' The acts performed with a consenting woman during love-making are not impure, according to Joseph. I would swear he was in good faith, convinced he was not breaking the Law.

This was how he reasoned: What are the commandments worrying about? That you do not lay hands on a woman if she belongs to someone else. If the law-giver had meant to prohibit the pleasures of the flesh he would have ordered: 'Thou shalt not desire woman.' And if he had wanted everything to be contained in marriage, he would have completed the sentence by saying: 'Thou shalt not covet a woman who is not thy wife.' But instead he confined himself to 'Thou shalt not covet thy neighbour's wife.' No girls, therefore, because they belong to their parents or to their future husband, who has a right to demand their virginity; and no wives, because they belong to their husbands. And that leaves widows.

This demonstration, which to Joseph seemed severely logical, had been expounded to me many times, with variants, comments and glosses based on personal experience of the speaker. Now my master, when I tried to get him started on his favourite subject, answered me with irritation.

'Have you seen Maria lately?' he asked me. 'You haven't. Then go and see her.'

I obeyed him. From the impression that the new Maria made on me I could guess at the impression made on him.

Now I knew where Joseph went when, at any hour of the day, he left the shop and went down to the main street, below; he passed the house of Cleophas, then went behind it, to glance over the low wall of the garden. He never saw her: Maria led a very sheltered life.

She was a solitary girl, with no friends. She was never to be seen standing in the midst of a group, bending her head to the head of some girl-friend, to whisper and laugh, or walking alone with another girl her age, making that special sign of a finger raised to her lips, the gesture that accompanies confidences and requests secrecy.

Joseph, too, was alone. A man who appeals too greatly to women cannot count on the solidarity of other males. And my master had, unintentionally, defied too much the susceptibility and envy of other youths: he with his fine horse; he beloved and desired by all women; he the protagonist of so many adventures, whether real or invented. Now that he was on foot they all made him pay for the past. If he went to the tavern nobody would drink or dice with him; in the synagogue he was never asked to read a passage of Scripture or to take part in a discussion.

* * *

Another consequence of the encounter with Maria was a sudden cooling in Joseph's relations with Dorothea, who for two years had been his mistress. Listlessness, a melancholy, dreaming love led him to see her less and less.

Their affair was secret; even I, who should have been aware of it, did not even faintly suspect it for months, though Joseph received the lady in the shed where we seasoned the wood, only a few paces from my shed. Sometimes, when I went there to pull out an old log, I was surprised by the perfume that hovered in the room, which was surely not the smell of olive or acacia wood. I shook my head, accusing myself of evil thoughts. And, actually, the love-bower was just behind there, reached by shifting a beam and proceeding beyond the woodpiles. Joseph had arranged a makeshift pallet and, when he expected a visit in the night, he would put a few drops of a sleeping-draught in my wine.

He would have preferred even me to remain ignorant of the woman who came to him and of her identity; I understood why when, by chance, I saw her one night, almost at the break of dawn. I had drunk no wine the previous evening because I did not feel well, and so I awoke very early. In the vague glow I was surprised to see, coming from the shed cautiously, her head veiled, the beautiful Dorothea, widow of the rich man. I recognized her by her tall, slim figure, her golden apparel, the elegant sandals that enclosed her delicate little feet.

There had been only one rich man in the city, Antonius Rufus, the merchant, who had Latinized his name the better to swim with the tide of Romans who were invading the world. He had risen from nothing. A wandering pedlar at sixteen, he took to the women of the inland towns the refined goods of the big cities: purple tunics from Sidon, bolts of byssus, gold rings, carpets. In partnership with a Greek, he had set up a shop selling refined and rare things: felt caps, sandals from Laodicea, inlaid caskets, painted vases. At twenty-five he owned a whole bazaar. At fifty, he was in control of a great business network: he would settle for a year in a distant city, set up a sales organization, and then come back to feed, from the land of Israel, the new commercial outlets.

Nazareth was his native city, where he returned for brief periods of rest. He owned a large house in the same street as the house of Cleophas. And there he had died, shortly after

Joseph's arrival in the city. He left a widow, a young Greek with very white skin and blond hair, who was treated with great respect because she was never seen in public and had no women friends. She was held up as an example to young girls: she stayed at home, the picture of modesty; she aided the poor, who came into her courtyard the day before the Sabbath; and she did not even go to the synagogue, as she did not worship the god of Israel. Loneliness ravaged her, like a disease.

Joseph had desired only one woman in Nazareth: Dorothea. He had never seen her, but the fame of her beauty and her shyness had sufficed to inflame him. One day he joined with the poor. She appeared in the loggia to greet her beneficiaries, with a queen's graciousness. Joseph saw her; and he was seen. When the poor withdrew, my master pretended to go out with them and hid inside a stone ark at the end of the court. At the hour of repose, in the afternoon, when the house seemed dead, he lifted the heavy lid and climbed to the upper rooms. He dared present himself in Dorothea's chamber! He was not driven out, but he was not received, either. On his death-bed Antonius Rufus had made his wife vow that she would never receive men in his house, and Dorothea was determined to keep this vow. So that first day all they did was agree as to how and when they would see each other again: the two loneliest people in Nazareth had met.

From our yard you could see the highest storey of Dorothea's house: a red cloth flapping among the laundry hung out on the roof to dry was the signal that the lady would come to Joseph that same night. She came two or three times a week, very late, and went back home before dawn. Nazareth, at night, is a sleeping city and Dorothea ran no risk of being seen or of waking the dogs. She proceeded through the vast garden that extended behind her house, then appeared in the high road. She crossed it, and after a few steps entered our yard, not by the gate but through a crack in the wall beneath the figtree, where a person can get through sideways. She respected her vow and, in addition, experienced a thrill that prepared her senses for love.

Over a period of two years their love had never known weariness. Dorothea was tender, affectionate, capricious, Greek (which means she was knowing and refined), and she had known how to invade Joseph's senses if not his heart. Now the pace of their encounters began to slow.

As a rule I stood at a crack between the planks of my shed simply to see Dorothea arrive and leave: even covered and veiled, she was a joy for the eyes. So I noticed that, as soon as she left, my master also came out. He seemed to be following her: she disappeared, entering the postern of her garden; but Joseph took the little alley of steps that joined our street with the main one, just below, that passed before the house of Cleophas.

He did not pause, did not raise his eyes to the windows; he just walked past. Then he came home to sleep a couple of hours before beginning the day.

I believe that my master attended the Nazareth synagogue only for the pleasure of glimpsing for a moment the girls' faces among the folds of their veils, feeling their nearness even though they had to stay in the area set aside for them, and hearing them whisper, pray, sing. Many he didn't know; some were ugly; but it made no difference. Joseph had no specific intentions; he didn't want to make their acquaintance, or, least of all, have to acknowledge them the next day in the street. He desired only to remain immersed in this atmosphere of feminine scents, murmurs, rustlings, sandals clacking against tender heels, slim hands holding the prayer-shawl to the head. He liked to hear the unripe voices of the girls and the soft, chanting voices of the women, reciting the familiar prayer: 'Hear, O Israel: the Eternal One is our God . . . ' Now he went there chiefly to see Maria again: I could tell from the way he lingered at the entrance until she had arrived, or how he waited after the service until she came out with the other women. Still he insisted on ignoring what was happening to him; some evenings later, in the yard, he said to me: 'The day I fall in love, really, hopelessly, in love, will be the end of everything. A world made up of thousands of women would be reduced to just one woman. Can you imagine a worse fate for me?'

He winked, so that it would be clear he was joking; but I realized that he had begun to suffer for love; and it was the first time.

Maria had retained her childish grace. She left the house

rarely, always with her aunt or with her old nurse, dressed in black, her head bowed; but every now and then her disobedient eyes would slide away and look at things and people; and her sedate walk would break into little skips and dashes. In my opinion, when she was beside her nurse, a heavy and aggressive woman who did not so much walk as march, Maria could hardly resist tripping her up.

All the same, the sight of her had a devastating effect on Joseph. I saw this for myself one day when he happened to run into her on the market street, and I was with him. She greeted him in a straightforward way: 'The Lord be with you, Joseph,' and she smiled at him; she nodded at me with a smile. I was intent on looking at my master: he had neither blushed nor blanched. He stood still, with an almost painful concentration, not daring to raise his eyes to her. He answered her greeting mechanically and looked at her only when she and her nurse were far off, two black dots against the white of the walls. The next day Maria came to the shop. Joseph greeted her awkwardly, stammering; he blushed and retired to the other end of the bench to use the plane. I took her order because, from the way she was behaving, it was obvious she had come to us only as a customer. She wanted a nuptial chest, the kind in which a bride's outfit is kept.

'Are you getting married, Maria?' I asked her, winking.

'Perhaps,' she answered, with great detachment.

She never smiled in the whole half-hour she stayed there, explaining to me how the chest should be made, with what fittings and handles, how high the feet were to be and how they were to be shaped by the lathe, the kind of wood to be used, mortised and without nails. Little by little Joseph had turned, so that he could see her out of the corner of his eye, but he maintained the attitude of someone concentrating entirely on his work.

When she had gone, he raised the plane and hurled it to the end of the room.

It was at this very period that Joseph's social position rose rapidly: at the synagogue and in the street many greeted him before he could greet them; respectable mothers forgot about his amorous adventures (a young man's wild oats) and considered him a good match for their daughters, even those women who lived in the two-storey houses only the well-off inhabited. At twenty-five Joseph was now obliged to take a wife; as a rule a man starts a family at eighteen, and the doctors of the Law insist that the Almighty, blessed be his name, curses those who, at the age of twenty, are not yet married.

The source of all this respect was, naturally, money. For years Nathan had cut logs in the woods, and we had begun trading in wood, selling dressed and seasoned beams; our work in the shop was increasing; the house was entirely paid for. Old Elias, otherwise known as Mortise, our rival carpenter, was dead; his sons had quarrelled over the inheritance, and were still quarrelling to decide which of them had to stop drinking and start working. We were seriously thinking of hiring a couple of apprentices.

The proof that Joseph was now considered an influential person, worthy of representing the community, came when he was invited to take part in the Sabbath afternoon meetings. On the day set aside for rest, in the house of study next to the synagogue, under the leadership of the rabbi and of Judge Cleophas, the wisest and most authoritative citizens gathered to debate questions of theology: about twenty of the older men and one or two promising youths, like Joseph. All, or almost all, had wives, whom they told, with great urging of secrecy, what had been said in the meeting; so that the next day the whole city knew everything.

The subject of the debate, on the day Joseph took part in it, was the observance of the Sabbath rest. In Nazareth not only did people leave their houses without any necessity, but also for years they had developed the habit of strolling in the square. According to Cleophas, this was a clear demonstration that morals were lax and that, in Galilee, there was a widespread lack of religious severity. It is written that on the Sabbath no one shall walk more than six stadia, and as a rule the strollers did not go beyond that figure. But Cleophas had a great deal to say about the profane, even wicked purpose of those strolls.

Nazareth does not have a central square like Greek or Roman cities; before the lower gate, where the city touches the valley, a great square space opens, with no gardens or fountains in it. All around are shops and warehouses, because the gate is the most frequent place of access to the city and nearly all merchandise passes through it. On the Sabbath, at an hour of the afternoon that varied according to the seasons so that it would be neither too hot nor too cool, the young girls escorted by their mothers and the young men escorted by nobody would take three or four turns around the open area, the males in one direction, the females in the other. They looked and were looked at.

The turns around the square, as you can see, fulfilled a social function. Love, even engagements resulted. No matter how tempted a girl was, she rarely responded to the glances of a boy that her family would have considered undesirable. Accustomed to being in awe of their parents, reasonable perforce, the young maidens allowed themselves, here too, to be guided by those mysterious but very clear signals sent by their mothers walking beside them.

According to Cleophas this custom was to be abandoned: the stroll might not be against the letter of the law perhaps, but it surely profaned the spirit of the law. When he had finished his discourse, Cleophas urged those present to express their views. When Joseph's turn came, he summed up his objections in these three words: 'Genesis, one, twenty-two.'

The rabbi quoted the verse of Scripture to which Joseph had referred for those who might not have remembered it: 'Be fruitful, and multiply.' The holy man was, like my master, also in favour of the stroll. 'It is true,' he said, 'that marriages are arranged for the most part by the parents, but it is right that the young people should also have a way of seeing each other and knowing each other. What more chaste way is there for them to see and know each other than the Sabbath stroll? There are no baths here and no palestras,' he continued, 'where, in other countries, young men meet girls, all of them scantily dressed or completely naked, in a horrible promiscuity that common modesty forbids me to describe . . . And should we then abolish the Sabbath stroll?'

Those present agreed with him and Joseph, and the group did not condemn the Sabbath stroll, which in Nazareth is called 'the dogs' circle', because the dogs, sniffing at doorways from shop to shop, cover the perimeter of the same square, in their expeditions in search of food.

My master's first appearance in public was a success: with those words he earned the respect of the elders, the gratitude of all the city's bachelors and of all the girls of marriageable age.

The following Sabbath afternoon, as Joseph was obeying the precept of enforced repose (as he was blissfully asleep, in other words), a group of youths started calling him from the street: they invited him to join in the stroll, which he had defended at the synagogue meeting so effectively. They were a jolly, noisy bunch, whose respect for the Sabbath did not prevent them from laughing and shouting. Joseph went down and was welcomed among them like an old friend, even if they were all younger than he.

They lowered their voices and assumed a more staid demeanour when they reached the square: the stroll had a ritual aspect and a practical purpose that demanded gravity and attention. The two slow lines of males and females circulated in opposing directions making no sounds beyond quick whispers and the scrape of sandals. My master, who was witnessing this sight for the first time, was struck by it: the procession contradicted its religious composure only with the flash of looks and smiles, when the two groups passed each other.

He realized that the girls were smiling at him meaningfully; some female heads turned after he had gone by and the murmuring of mothers was heard, recalling their unruly daughters to order. Finally the women could gaze easily at the man of their dreams. It was not the first time they were seeing him, but now they could look at him in every detail. They admired Joseph's physical elegance and strength, the handsome and likeable face, but also his elegance of dress, his Greek hair-style. From his journeys to Ptolemais Joseph had brought back short tunics of embroidered silk, Syrian sashes and belts, footgear glittering with gold, cloaks of smooth wool from Tyre or from Sarepta. Nazareth had never seen a man better dressed, or one more handsome.

It seemed nevertheless, to Joseph that the girls were amused to see him walking in a circle with the other youths, as if this were a reason to make fun of him.

Not long afterwards Eliseus appeared at our house. The marriage-broker was a bearded, austere old man, with an air of authority that seemed borrowed, or rather put on in the morning along with his cloak before he went out, and put off, folded away, on his return home. It was known that his wife maltreated him, chasing him with her broom, so Eliseus could display a certain sternness only when he was well away from his domestic walls.

Circumspectly, with long turns of phrase, and in the end with the calculated shamelessness of a salesman, the broker presented his goods; and it was not a question of just one girl. When Joseph refused to hear the virtues of Abigail, daughter of Mordecai, the man started talking of the wealth of Noemi, daughter of Benjamin; and then of Susanna, daughter of Samuel the merchant; and of Martha, daughter of Nehemiah. It was perhaps the first time that Eliseus found himself acting for so many different girls, or rather for their parents, with the same man.

Joseph barely knew the girls of Nazareth, the names that the broker mentioned did not call up faces, forms. He submitted to that avalanche of offers, rather frightened; he looked around like a man seeking an avenue of escape. He finally asked the old man to what he owed this sudden and over-abundant crop of matrimonial offers, and he learned that it was his own fault. Unwisely taking part in the Sabbath stroll, he had offered himself as husband, according to the custom, and so he should not then be surprised that he had been taken seriously. He realized that the youths of the city had played a joke on him, drawing him into the square: they had assigned him a role of matrimonial candidate, and had taken their revenge on his superior airs, the horse, and the amorous successes in Ptolemais. But they had behaved with style, a quality my master appreciated, and he did not take offence. Indeed, he laughed and said: 'You can lead an ass to the trough but you cannot force him to drink. They led me to the stroll, but they cannot force me to marry. I will not go back again.'

He went back a few months later, when Maria, on a Sabbath afternoon, was accompanied by her aunt to 'the dogs' circle'.

When he learned that Maria was exposed to perusal in the square, Joseph was struck with grief and amazement. He was well aware that Maria had become a woman and in fact he gazed at her with ever-increasing perturbation the few times he encountered her; but he had chiefly retained the image of her that his recollections prompted: that of a little girl on tiptoe, a little dark head peering over the windowsill.

When the Sabbath came, Joseph fell in with the youths, who looked at him ironically, and he began his turns around the square. Maria noticed at once and smiled, but not at him; she was determined, on the contrary, to enjoy herself secretly, as if a foreseen and long-awaited event had finally occurred. Joseph, in fact, had eyes only for her. With what little remained of his attention, he kept an eye on the boys who looked at her, their signs and their smiles.

It did not cross his mind that, if her uncle and aunt had really wanted to find her a husband, they would have had ways to present to Maria the ideal suitors, of good family and good education, even young men from other cities, without forcing her to this exhibition. He didn't know that Maria herself had been the one to insist, until her aunt finally agreed to escort her. The girl's excuse had been her curiosity: she, too, wanted to see the famous 'dogs' circle'. When her relatives opposed her request, she declared that she would go in any case: escorted, if her aunt would decide to satisfy her; otherwise, alone. Synedrion, on this occasion, had had an access of authority, shouting, demanding the respect that was his due. When he had either to affirm his will and prevent Maria's plan (this was certainly possible, but it would have cost him endless sulks and spite, of which he was terrified) or else of accepting the consent that was imposed on him and passing it off as an act of generosity on his part, he chose this latter alternative and solemnly granted his permission.

The first time, nothing happened. Joseph, ignorant of the established signals with which the male and female strollers exchanged messages, did not understand what a dozen youths wanted to communicate to Maria, but it was not hard for him to imagine. It was harder for him to catch and interpret the girl's answers, as she moved her fingers and hands, barely smiling.

The following Sabbath he waited until a bold youth named Joel emerged from the stroll, the son of a man who hired out wagons. Joseph arranged to meet the youth outside the walls next morning when, as the Sabbath would be over, they could devote themselves to some violent physical exercise. It had seemed to Joseph that Joel, a young giant whose feet, according to rumour, stank horribly, had addressed insistent and indiscreet signs to Maria, or rather, the smiles Maria sent him in reply had seemed to Joseph too promising.

They met the next morning along the walls, outside the city; and Joseph realized it was true - Joel's feet stank. This fact made him indulgent: a girl like Maria could never have tolerated near her such a source of stench. They beat each other about for a while: the other youth was very big but lacked agility, so Joseph knocked him down before Joel could mar his face.

'Would you mind telling me why you wanted this fight?' Joel asked, still on the ground. And as Joseph did not answer, he added: 'If it's because of the judge's niece, she's fair game. I'm trying my luck.'

'No,' Joseph said, 'not you. Not any of you.'

'You want to marry her yourself?'

'No,' Joseph answered. 'I'm not going to get married, but all of you are to leave Maria alone.'

This line of reasoning seemed cockeyed to Joel, outright arrogance in fact. He got to his feet and continued fighting with Joseph. The only result was a bruise on my master's cheekbone and a broken rib for Joel. Then the pair swore they harboured no hostile feelings towards each other; indeed, they would be friends from then on, Joseph insisted, provided that Feet gave up any interest in Maria. Again, this condition seemed going too far for Joel, and they resumed their brawl. The epic fight lasted, with occasional interruptions to catch breath, almost the whole day. Nathan and I arrived as soon as we were alerted: sunset was near and on the slope below the wall a good half of the male population of Nazareth had gathered. In living memory there had never been such a fight in the city or its environs.

Joel was bleeding fairly badly and his friends finally took him home on a cart; Joseph walked, with Nathan and me supporting him. He too was bleeding, but his face, as the mirror soon confirmed, had barely been touched. Reassured as to the condition of his beauty, my master was treated, and he lay down on his bed. He seemed very satisfied. He himself could not have said why this duel had appeased him, why it seemed to him a virile action as well as a clear expression of his entangled feelings. He stayed in bed two days.

When she learned of the fight, Maria vented her annoyance to her aunt. 'That fool,' she said, 'what does he think he's doing? Is he going to challenge all the boys who smile at me, one after the other? He'll get his face broken and he won't be so handsome any more.' Someone had repeated to her what Joseph had said about not wanting to marry her, and she had said to herself: He'll pay for that.

But the next day, as if she just happened to be passing, she came to the window of the shop and enquired about my master's health. She would not come in, but lingered for a long chat with me and with Nathan. She said she could not understand how two sensible people like Joel and Joseph could brawl for no reason.

There is a reason, Nathan said to her with gestures; he is as ingenuous as he is dumb sometimes.

'I don't know the reason why they acted like savages,' Maria answered, in absolute bad faith, 'but nothing could be worth hitting each other like that.'

The fight made a deep impression on the other rivals of my master. They had believed that Joseph, simply because he combed his hair Greek-style and wore silk, had no guts; and yet, on the contrary, he had beaten up Joel who was the biggest and strongest amongst them. They all decided to ignore Maria during the Sabbath stroll. They kept their word; and she was very irritated.

Joseph met her, out walking with her nurse, and went up to her with a smug smile: he felt he deserved her thanks for having fought over her. A smile from her would have been sufficient response. Maria allowed him to approach and, when he came within range, she gave him two slaps, one on each side, hard and sharp. She turned and went off.

Joseph had to think a moment before he managed to understand that the girl did not appreciate brawls in her name. In particular she did not appreciate his fighting for her as he was shouting that he did not want to marry her.

Another person also felt that the fight between Joseph and Joel concerned her, and this was Dorothea who, having hung the red cloth on her terrace, saw from her window the axe, that was our sign, hanging with the handle down; and this signal meant that she was not to come. The signal of prohibition remained there for a week; then they met again, she and Joseph, and they spent the night together. Dorothea had come to make a jealous scene, but instead she found herself suggesting plans for the future: how to go on seeing each other when Joseph was married. Because he would have to marry, sooner or later, wouldn't he? Dorothea did not fear rivals: no crude Galilean girl, with calluses on her feet and a short tunic below her knees, would take Joseph from her.

VIII

Joseph grew a beard. I shaved regularly, in the Roman way; but the men of Israel followed a different tradition: they were bearded and wore their hair long. My master's beard, short and neatly trimmed, was less dark than his hair, almost blond.

In Galilee spring is a very green season. Around Nazareth the hills and the little valleys between them burst out with wild grasses. Bushes force their way towards the sun, outstripping the less hardy plants and forming, with them, inextricable tangles. Joseph would go out walking through the fields, gathering great bunches of flowers, but before reentering the city, he would throw them away.

His walk always took place towards sunset, after he had finished working. One day, as he was coming home, he went past Cleophas's garden and he was overcome by a sudden impulse: he leaped over the low wall, walked among the tamarisks and laurels that bordered the paths through the beds of vegetables, then on through the apple trees and the jujubes, the roses and the saffron-coloured crocuses, amidst the aromas of that exuberance of plants, to the cistern where rain-water was collected for watering the garden in summer. He looked up at the house, which could just be glimpsed, half-hidden by the olives and the figs; then he sighed and sat down on the edge of the cistern, his back to the house.

Maria had seen him from her room on the upper floor, its window overlooking the garden; and she came down, carrying a little basket. She was meant to seem the dutiful daughter, coming out to gather vegetables; but from her dress you would have thought she was going to an open-air party. She had combed her hair, binding it with a yellow ribbon; in place of her simple tunic, she had put on a pleated sleeveless garment that came from Alexandria, woven of finest white linen, its hem embroidered with golden thread. She wore a girdle of soft leather, yellow like her hair-ribbon. On her bare feet were new sandals of very fine jackal-hide, in yellow and purple stripes. Joseph had never seen her dressed like a grown lady; when he turned, at the rustle of her step, he remained motionless with surprise and was unable to say a word.

Maria did not greet him. She pretended to be irritated at finding an intruder, and asked Joseph what he was doing there in the garden. Her voice was cold, her manner stern: at that moment my master realized she had truly become a woman.

'Never mind,' he said, also with an edge of irritation in his voice. 'Don't you remember that I knew you when you were only so high?'

'What of that?'

'Don't put on such airs. We're friends, or at least we used to be. Can't you realize that I might want to have a talk with you, as we did in the old days? Really, I don't know anything about you now; nor do you know anything about me. I have no idea what you want, what you think . . . '

The girl put her right foot forward, as if to break into a run; then she began by saying: 'What would you suggest then? Should you hide again in my uncle's garden like a thief? Or would it be more convenient for you if I came to your shop and ruined my reputation before the whole city? Haven't you learned the rules? If you want to see me, come to the Sabbath stroll, like the others.'

'The others,' Joseph murmured. 'There won't be any others.'

'How dare you hit my suitors? They behave honestly at least. They do want to marry me . . . '

'But you see . . . I . . . ' Joseph muttered, embarrassed.

'You had the nerve to declare publicly that you don't want to marry me. What will people think?'

'After all,' he rebutted, 'nobody can force me. If I don't want to, I don't want to, and that's that.'

'Fine. But meanwhile you prevent anyone else from asking for my hand. What can they think? That you still have some claim to me, that you're my lover, for example . . . And I won't have that. I'm a respectable girl.'

'I know,' Joseph murmured, downcast. 'I know, and I

respect you.' He had sunk again to a sitting position, his back against the cistern. 'But I need you,' he went on, his voice intense, 'I want to see you again.'

'What for?'

'To talk to you, to be with you . . . ' Joseph didn't dare say more.

'If you don't want me to be your wife, what could I ever be for you?'

'I don't know,' he answered, hesitating. 'A companion, a friend. Two people don't have to be married in order to be fond of each other. I would respect you . . . '

'Nonsense. You know that any friendship between man and woman is impossible outside of marriage,' she said, repeating a deeply-rooted opinion as if it were an obvious truth.

'Well then,' Joseph replied, 'do you want me to marry you? Is that why you're so angry?'

'Me?!' she cried, an emphatic question, as if the very notion of marrying Joseph were enough to fill her with shocked amazement. 'You're mistaken, my friend. I wouldn't marry you if you were the only man left in this city. What's got into your head?'

'That's what I meant,' Joseph answered, stiffly. 'Then it won't matter to you if I don't get married. But you should act the same, like a true friend. I won't marry, and you won't marry either.'

Maria didn't bother to explain to him why such a bargain was out of the question. 'Would that be enough for you?' she asked, with feigned sweetness.

My master sighed, then said: 'I'd make it be enough.'

'And does that seem to you the proper way for a man to act?' the girl blurted. 'Shame on you! I'd stay a virgin and a spinster, while you would console yourself with the trollops of Ptolemais. No, no, my dear. All too easy for you . . . '

Joseph stood up and faced her. 'I can't,' he murmured painfully. 'I can't get married. For me, marriage would be like a disease . . . an incurable disease . . . '

'Like the plague . . . ' Maria prompted him.

'Or leprosy . . . '

'Then keep away from me, or you'll be infected,' the girl cried and slapped his face, before she turned and went towards the house again, not looking back.

Joseph stood there a long time, his hand on his cheek. He came home in a grim mood, and as he passed the gate, he turned the axe so its handle was down, in order that Dorothea would stay in her own house that night.

Maria, too, was anything but pleased with herself. She had no girl-friends intimate enough to be told what had happened, and so she unburdened herself to an old doll that had lost almost all its stuffing of chaff. Still not consoled, she sought out her aunt, but said to her only, 'I gave him a slap.' Then she burst into tears. Her aunt took Maria on her lap, rocked her as if she were a baby; and Maria at last fell asleep.

Joseph had never seen Maria dressed so well; he had never seen her hair, usually concealed by a shawl or a veil. She had looked to him like a great lady, but at the same time no different from that stubborn child he had known, frank and determined, prompt to defend her rights, even using her hands. It was a great pity she was so beautiful and could be had only with marriage.

He could not forget the little hand that had touched him, even if it was only to give him a slap. He even avoided Dorothea: the axe-handle remained stubbornly in the downward position.

On two successive Sabbaths, at the afternoon stroll, he addressed to Maria the signal that means 'can I see you again?' which consists of hooking the index finger. It was only at the second signalling that she condescended to answer yes by furtively moving her finger in the same way.

They met the following afternoon at the cistern in the garden. Maria was bare-foot, wearing an old tunic; she hadn't even put a ribbon in her hair. She wanted to show herself in her humblest array, without the allure of her fine dress. Actually she was running no risk: he found her more beautiful than ever. Straightforward and proud in her worn tunic, Maria seemed to him even more intimidating than in her great lady's attire.

Joseph was a bit ill-at-ease because, as he was waiting for her, he had leaned against the brimming cistern and had wet the front of his tunic. The soaked cloth now made his erection evident. He bent forward slightly so the tunic would not cling to his body.

Unexpectedly, Maria was meek and sweet. She began by asking his pardon.

'For what?' Joseph said, sincerely: for he had forgotten about the slap.

'Why, for having struck you, my dear,' she said, running her hand over his cheek in a brief caress. 'It was silly and impulsive of me.'

'Maybe it's because you're a bit fond of me,' he ventured, 'and you don't have the courage to say so.'

'How could I help but be fond of you, Joseph? You've been dear to me ever since I was a little girl, when I first met you, in Bethlehem, in the yard of the inn, and you treated me like a grown-up, an equal. I've never forgotten that.' Filled with emotion, her voice paused for a moment, then resumed in a different tone: 'But now that I am grown up, you treat me as if I were a child, or an inferior.'

'That's not true,' Joseph protested. He had come closer to her and was holding her hand. Maria withdrew it.

'It is true,' the girl said. 'You don't want to marry me, but you create scandal around my name. You want to keep your freedom but rob me of mine. You come to see me; and I'm not the only woman you talk of love with. I'm sure of that. You treat me like a cheap girl, an unimportant friend.'

Joseph remained silent.

'I can't share you with other women, Joseph. I have to be enough for you, as you would be enough for me.'

'What do you want me to do?'

'Think about it, and you'll see for yourself what you should do. But don't come to see me again until you know.'

Weighed down by the decisions he would have to make, as he saw a changed life opening before him, Joseph dug at the ground with the tip of his sandal.

'I love you,' Maria said, in a whisper. With a sudden movement, she flung her arms around him and kissed him on the mouth. She pressed her lips to his hard, like a seal; then they found the sweetness of a less violent contact. Joseph responded with passion, clasping her to him, with a long sigh. What he had longed for, and had believed impossible, was taking place: Maria was giving him a true kiss, a kiss of love.

Suddenly she broke free and ran towards the house.

'Me, too!' Joseph shouted after her. 'I love you, too.'

He lingered a little longer beside the cistern; he tried to hold on to the sweet and burning sensation of that kiss, no longer worrying about the definitive words that had been addressed to him.

He began to think about them that evening, after supper, alone on the roof of the house. The alternative that faced him was a torment: marrying Maria meant giving up the others, giving up Dorothea, and Daniel's Maria, and Abigail, Naomi, Susannah, Martha, all yearning for him. And more, it meant dismissing from his life the variety and the vicinity of the feminine world, the very thought of the infinite possible adventures, of love as a tender game; he would have to sacrifice what for him was like a second sunlight. Joseph didn't think, except for a moment perhaps, about being an unfaithful husband.

He could give up Maria. Or could he, really? As time went by, the more he felt drawn towards her. He saw her again and again, in her elegant dress, and then with bare feet but elegant even in her old tunic. He saw her eyes, her smile. From her he had received only some slaps, a caress, and one kiss; and he could not forget the hand, the lips, that had touched him. As he recalled these, he was so caught up in the memory that all thought of the other women dwindled and faded, and only Maria existed. Then he gave himself a shake, shivering as if he were on the brink of an abyss; and he filled his head with other images, in which other smiles gleamed, and Dorothea held him in her arms.

Two evenings later he turned the axe-handle to the upward position, signalling the Greek woman to come; and he clung to her, since she could mean his rescue. But in the love of Dorothea he no longer found the old spell.

A few more days went by, then one evening Joseph talked with me, confiding in me the things I have just told. This was a serious symptom, because my master was somewhat reserved about his love affairs, distrustful. Perhaps he decided to do this now only for the pleasure of talking about Maria with somebody who knew her.

That period of private conflict destroyed his peace of mind and consumed his flesh as well. Thin, nervous, my master no longer seemed himself. He quarrelled with me and even addressed harsh words to Nathan: something he had never done before. He pined but he still wouldn't give up; he spent sleepless nights, but he held fast. One evening he went to the tavern and got drunk: this was perhaps the only way to dispel for a few hours the thoughts that besieged him. It was a lonely drunkenness: Joseph drank a great amount of wine, seated, grim and determined, in a corner of the squalid room, until he crumpled to the floor. They sent for me and I collected him and brought him home, dragging him some of the way, carrying him on my back the rest of the time. He slept the whole next day.

Two weeks had gone by since his last meeting with Maria, when my master went back to the garden and waited for the girl beside the cistern. She saw him from her room, because she was keeping watch there evening after evening; but she did not come down immediately. She kept him waiting a long time, restraining herself with difficulty from running to meet him.

Finally she arrived at the place where Joseph, leaning on the cistern with one hand, was learning how to be patient; and she greeted him with the usual words: 'The Lord be with you.' He didn't give her time to finish even the short sentence; he began at once to say what he had come for: 'Yes, I'll marry you. All right, I agree; I'll marry you.' His voice was clear and strong; he wanted to commit himself, to make sure he couldn't go back on his declaration.

He was expecting Maria to fling her arms around his neck, picking up where they had left off the last time. But she didn't move; she replied: 'This is usually what the girl says when her hand is asked in marriage. Unless she says no. So far there's been no word about me. One day you declare in public you won't marry me; another day you insist that you will. Do you think you can use me just as you please?'

Joseph was bewildered; he couldn't understand what more the girl could want of him. He said to her: 'I don't understand.'

Maria came to his aid. 'Have you come to ask me to marry you?'

'Yes,' Joseph said, his teeth clenched.

'Then do it, and I'll answer you.'

My master was already beginning to lose his privileges: it was no longer a matter of bestowing himself, like a prize, but of setting himself on the same plane as a woman, something he had never thought he would have to do. He looked at her: Maria had put on a less worn tunic than the previous time and was wearing clogs on her feet. She was dressed, in other words, as she used to dress when she really did come down to pick vegetables in the garden. In its way, this attire was also a demonstration: not showy and not shabby, it was saying Maria wanted him to see her in everyday guise.

'What a lot of fuss,' Joseph grumbled. 'What more do you want?'

Maria didn't answer him.

'I said I would marry you,' he went on, 'because I know you'll say yes. If the answer was going to be no, you'd have given me the idea already.' He hesitated still. 'Do I actually have to ask you?'

Maria remained silent.

'Will you marry me?' Joseph said finally, swallowing his words a bit.

As if to reward him for the effort he had made, she kissed him on the mouth, stepped back for a moment, then kissed him again. Joseph responded with ardour. Maria broke off, to ask him: 'Before you came here to ask me your question, did you make sure you were free of all ties with other women?'

'No,' he admitted.

'Then how can you ask me to marry you, to promise to love you and be faithful to you, when you've shared another woman's bed until yesterday and perhaps have let her believe that all will go on between the two of you as before even after you're married?'

'No, not that,' Joseph said. 'I will be faithful to you.'

'Then come back when you're free and ask me again. The Lord be with you.'

Maria went back towards the house without touching him, though he had held out his hands several times, to meet hers, but had frozen each time, seeing that she showed no sign of wanting to respond to him.

Joseph didn't know how to break things off with Dorothea painlessly. In the end he faced her indignation, practically speaking disarmed, because he could offer her no logical reason for the break, except the fact that he was about to be married;

and the Greek woman, beyond any doubt, would not have found that a good reason at all.

When she saw that Joseph was greeting her in the low-ceilinged room next to the shop, instead of in the shed, the woman understood immediately and allowed him to explain, in a harsh voice at times then stammering, his intention of getting married.

'Are you going to be a faithful husband, dear?' she asked him, with a hint of derision. 'Will you close your eyes to things like this?' and she opened her dress to bare her bosom, which was very beautiful. Joseph looked down at the ground, and she started laughing.

A little later Dorothea left my master's house, but before going off, she offered him her sympathy: 'Poor boy, you could have been the happiest of men among women, seated in a court of mistresses, like a prince of Arabia, and instead you go and bury yourself in the arms of a little Galilean girl. You'll swear to be faithful to her, and you'll regret it for the rest of your life.'

Free now and aware of what it meant to marry Maria, Joseph did not rush to Cleophas's garden for the final agreement. He was in no hurry, precisely because he felt the decisiveness of the words he would utter. He wanted to be quite sure of himself. He could anticipate the joy of taking Maria into his arms, of committing himself to her; he was ready for the sacrifice, but he was also reflecting on all that he was giving up, and he realized it was no small thing.

One evening, passing me in the yard, he gripped me by the shoulders and shook me. He had drunk a lot at table; there was wine on his breath. 'I can still say no,' he announced to me with that solemnity, that deep, slow voice, that drinkers usually assume when they're not yet totally drunk. Then he went to the well and emptied a bucket of water over his head.

He hesitated for another two days. Quiet and brooding, he spent the time on the roof, looking in the direction of the hills. Then he prayed, washed carefully, put on a white linen tunic, new sandals, bound his hair with two silk bands whose ends fell to his shoulders, and he entered the garden of Cleophas. Maria was already awaiting him at the cistern; she was pleased that he came to her, purified by water and prayer, dressed as if for a meeting at the synagogue. She was wearing a blue tunic, with a ribbon of the same colour in her hair. He and she both knew that this was the decisive encounter.

'Here I am,' Joseph said simply. 'And now, do you want to marry me?'

'Of course, Joseph. I will love you as long as I live.' Maria embraced her beloved and kissed him.

They sat down, side by side, to tell each other how much they were in love. My master discovered that love can also be peace and happiness, whereas for him it had mostly been struggle and uneasiness. Now he was pleased that he had resisted temptation a few nights earlier, with Dorothea. Now that the time of conflict was past, Maria was serene and tender; she wanted him to realize that he would be marrying a meek woman. She rested her head against his shoulder and repeated the words of the Song of Songs: 'Kiss me with the kisses of your mouth, for your love is better than wine'. Joseph kissed her and, continuing with the comparisons of the sacred text, he said that her hair was as a flock of goats that appeared from Mount Gilead, and her teeth like a flock of sheep just shorn, her lips like a thread of scarlet, and her cheeks like pieces of pomegranate.

The last simile was the only one that Maria appreciated, because there really is no pink more delicate and subtle than the colour of pomegranate seeds. But for Joseph she invented her own comparisons. She said his teeth were blanched almonds, and his lips were velvety poppy-flowers, and his hair was the water of a cascade at night. She touched his face with long dreamed-of gestures; she said she wanted to make sure it was hers. The girls of Nazareth would surely envy her, she knew that. 'But it's only right,' she said, 'that, of all the girls, I should have you.'

'Why?' Joseph asked.

'Because I saw you first.' She burst into soft laughter, and Joseph laughed with her.

At this point it should have been Joseph's strict duty to ask the girl's family for her hand and become officially betrothed: Maria would see him after that only in the house of Cleophas, with her aunt or her nurse present, until the moment of the wedding. But she begged him to wait. It would be so beautiful to keep their understanding a secret still for a few days, meeting in the cool garden without anyone's knowing. They had many things to say to each other, they had to fill the gap of years that had separated them.

It was obvious from Joseph's change of mood that something had happened to him: he sang as he worked, and towards evening he would go out, fast as a hare leaping from its nest. At the cistern he and Maria would talk about the future, the children that would be born to them; or about the past, and they would both be moved as they recalled the inn in Bethlehem or their first encounter in Nazareth, as Joseph wandered through the strange city in the company of Nathan and then Maria called to him from the door of her house. She made her lover jealous by telling him, as if they were only jokes, of the approaches of Joel, of Horeb known as Hen, of Tobias, of Azarias, and of Hur. When Joseph learned that Hur had also had a try, he was annoyed because the quarrelsome young bully was also good-looking.

Sensing Joseph's jealousy, Maria laughed with delight and teased him about his own past, his loves, his excursions to Ptolemais. She had a very vague idea of Joseph's adventures; she was jealous on principle, but felt no specific rivalry towards my master's girlfriends, remote now and foreign. She was more irritated by the innocent girls of her own age, Susanna, Martha, Rebecca, Michal, who directed their smiles at Joseph during the dog's circle. These girls she knew.

Joseph, wisely, told her nothing. He said that his other women belonged to the past and he had forgotten them. 'When I'm with you,' he said, 'they don't exist,' and it was almost the truth. In Maria he discovered a different sort of girl, innocent and mettlesome, who demanded respect for her ideas and would never be a victim, not even of the man she loved. All of this had fascinated him.

They kissed. It was Maria who took the initiative, gently holding his head in her hands and pressing her lips to his. These were chaste kisses, or so they seemed to Joseph, who was in a position to compare them to the kisses of expert and avid lovers. Carried away by the same wave of emotion, he embraced the girl wildly, held her tight, touched her even where her modesty had imposed a limit. Each time he tried to cross the tacit boundary she had set for their embraces, she would freeze, offended, and sit a bit farther away.

Joseph specifically enjoyed listening to her when she daydreamed about the future and could see two and even three generations of descendants, all handsome and God-fearing.

'Is it so important for them to be handsome?' he asked.

'It is inevitable.' She smiled. 'Because they'll be your children and grandchildren.'

At other times she seemed to be pursuing some thought that came into her mind, and Joseph, feeling suddenly abandoned, would ask her: 'What are you thinking about?'

'About you, my dear,' she answered. 'About your love. I would never be certain that you love me the way I want you to, not even if I were to enter inside you, if the two of us were to become one. But you will love me because I love you; you won't be able to escape it.'

Joseph shook his head, unused to examining emotions. She jokingly tugged at his beard, patted it, stroked it. 'I'll keep on,' she threatened him, laughing, 'until your beard purrs, like a cat.'

Once again they took part in the Sabbath stroll, so that no one would suspect that they had come to an understanding. Many signals and smiles were addressed to Maria, because the boys had regained courage and collectively defied Joseph. From the other ranks, many girls silently offered themselves to Joseph, who finally could take no more and left the square with a sigh, because his youth was ending along with his freedom.

That evening my master went to the tavern to bid a tacit farewell to his bachelor life. Perhaps wanting to start something, Hur made a bet with his friends that he would be the one who, in the end, would marry the judge's niece. He boasted of having his special personal methods of seduction, convinced that no girl could resist him. He made no reference to Joseph, who, aware that the boy's words were foolish bragging, paid no attention to him. My master had gone there with the idea of getting merrily drunk, celebrating his private holiday; but after a while the wine began to bore him and he came home.

That period, during which he enjoyed the privileges of a betrothal, without having assumed any official obligation, was about to end. Joseph knew that he had to go further, and with this idea of marriage he had to confront first of all me and Nathan, then Cleophas, and afterwards all the others.

Meanwhile he went on meeting Maria by the cistern, talking in a way that to him and to her seemed totally new, the way that all lovers talk.

One evening Maria asked him: 'Would you love me even if we had to be separated, perhaps even for a long time?'

Questions like this are, in fact, a part of the language of lovers, and Joseph knew that he had to say yes, even though he had no idea what effects a prolonged absence of Maria might have on him. In other words, he assumed it was just a conventional expression, not a real question. But it was real: Maria was talking about a genuine and imminent separation.

She wanted to go to the country near Jerusalem; to the house of her aunt Elizabeth, to be with her during the birth of a child, which was to arrive soon. For a long time the old woman had been praying to the Lord for a child. In her young womanhood and her mature years the prayer had not been answered. Only now had she become pregnant at an age when, as a rule, women have long since ceased to be fertile. It was an extraordinary event, and the child's birth, healthy and lively, would be an even greater wonder.

To be sure, old Elizabeth would need all possible assistance. Maria, impulsively generous, could already see herself at her aunt's side, relieving her of her tasks; she imagined herself saving the old woman's life. Joseph was opposed to the journey, for obvious reasons: unsafe roads, the girl's lack of experience, and therefore the uselessness of her inadequate and clumsy aid, not to mention the extreme impropriety of a young girl's undertaking such a journey by herself. Maria argued, made objections; he answered them, but without any great concern because he was sure the plan would never become reality. It was inconceivable that a young girl should stay several months away from home. Cleophas, the severe judge, the forbidding uncle and guardian, would take care to nip his niece's project in the bud.

Which only goes to show that Joseph didn't know Cleophas well, and didn't even know Maria well enough.

IX

For Eliseus, the marriage-broker, it was a pleasure to go and ask the hand of the judge's niece in Joseph's name. He had known Cleophas for a long time, and it seemed that the mission entrusted to him now did not involve any difficulties. Joseph was a good young man, a good catch, of good background: a son-in-law that no father in Nazareth would have refused. But, on the contrary, Cleophas showed no signs of enthusiasm.

It was not just the grudge he bore because of that night when he ended up in the red paint and the fox-trap in our yard; he had also accumulated a certain number of little hostile feelings towards Joseph, envy, jealousy, irritation at hearing the youth discussed so much at home and outside. The older man seemed to hate the younger. He was too shrewd to come out and say no openly. He said yes, but for the donation that the bridegroom was obliged to give to the bride's family he asked an excessive sum, which Joseph would never have been able to pay. Eliseus pleaded his case as best he could, reminding his authoritative fellow-citizen that the custom of donation was by now abandoned, and it was only among the barbarian nations that husbands still bought wives. But his words were futile. Cleophas was obstinate.

To be sure, he couldn't continue his opposition for long, with two women in the house in favour of the match, one with a lover's passion, the other with maternal enthusiasm for that marriage her husband would gladly have prevented. He held out through their scenes, bore with their jibes and sulks; but he broke down when Maria sat on his lap, as she had done as a little girl, and murmured to him that he shouldn't make her so unhappy.

Joseph had to pay a token donation, five silver shekels, so that Cleophas could appear to have won his point. Maria, who knew her Scriptures well, said to Joseph that she had cost him less than Jacob paid for his bride Rachel: the patriarch had served his master for seven years and in the end Laban tricked him and gave him his other daughter, Leah. Before he could have Rachel, Jacob was forced to work another seven years.

'Would you have waited fourteen years for me?' Joseph asked her.

'No,' she said, laughing. 'There would have been no point. In all those years I'd have become an old woman, and you wouldn't have wanted me any more.'

The contract was drawn up and, for the signing, Joseph entered the judge's house a second time. He was no longer overcome by shyness as he had been on the first occasion. He noticed that the house needed repainting, the furniture was old and in poor condition, the service barely adequate. Cleophas was not so rich as he seemed, and this thought heartened Joseph: he put up with the judge's aloof and haughty attitude, and was even amused by it. After all, he would be taking Maria to his own house to live, and her uncle would no longer have any authority over her.

Betrothal, among the people of Israel, is a serious matter, more so than in any other country where I've lived. I would even say it's a kind of marriage. The man can take his betrothed to his house and begin their conjugal life at any time; if a child is born during the period of engagement, it is considered legitimate; and it is not so long ago that a promised girl, if found unfaithful, was stoned to death. It is, however, considered good manners for the engaged couple to see each other as little as possible and for them to know only the duties of their new condition. To maintain the high tradition of his house and his own dignity as a judge (and also because of his now-doubled grudge against Joseph), Cleophas confined his niece within his walls, allowing her out to go to the synagogue, but only if accompanied by both his wife and himself.

This somewhat paradoxical situation was borne patiently by both the young people, who continued seeing each other secretly, in the garden. Seated by the cistern, the betrothed pair discussed important questions: whether Joseph was more handsome with his beard or without, the people to invite to the wedding feast, the name most suitable for their first-born son.

Maria liked solemn names, of kings and prophets: Saul,

Jeremiah, Baruch. Joseph, unlike most prospective fathers, wanted a girl and would call her Judith or Deborah. Maria suspected that this preference for a daughter and for a special couple of names concealed some regret: a girl that Joseph had loved, perhaps, and who had had that name. But he denied it all.

For a little while Maria continued her teasing, then she went on to provoke him in a different way, bringing up her obsession with the forthcoming journey to visit her aunt Elizabeth. In the end the young couple quarrelled, in the childish fashion, repeating their arguments without justifying them. 'You won't go,' he said. 'I will go,' she replied. One saying no and the other yes, they went on for quite a while until Maria burst into tears. Seeing her cry and feeling responsible were a single, immediate emotion for Joseph: he caressed her, consoled her. But he still felt he was right and, weary of falling back on the familiar reasons against the trip, he turned to the principle of authority: you won't leave because I say not to, and you've promised to obey me.

'I did? Never!'

'Yes, dear. When you agreed to be my wife, you became obliged to observe my wishes,' Joseph said to her, smiling.

His calm exasperated the girl, who was evaluating perhaps for the first time the condition of submission which she had vowed to accept. 'Even when you're wrong?' she stammered, about to cry again.

'But I'm right,' Joseph answered, convinced.

Maria went into a tantrum. She paced nervously around the cistern, her eyes blinded by anger. She stumbled over the onion patch. Joseph picked her up and let her release all her disappointment at the loss of her independence, as she sobbed and kicked. 'Stupid!' she said to him, hammering at his chest with her fists.

Joseph had extensive experience with angry women, and he took care not to argue with her. He drew her into his arms and held her tight until the sobs died away. Maria cried for a little white longer, quietly, her head against his shoulder. Then she murmured to him, 'You really don't want me to go away?'

'I can't be without you,' Joseph answered. 'If you're not here, I feel lost.' And he delicately stroked her hair. It was the truth: the girl was filling all the empty spaces in his life; she was a friend, a confidant, a companion in dreaming, and soon she would become a complete woman, his woman.

'Only one thing is keeping me here,' Maria answered, consoled: 'The thought that if I were to stay away a couple of months, you'd start looking at the other girls again.' But immediately afterwards, she added, in a joking tone: 'But I trust you, and I'll put you to the test.'

Though Joseph was completely unable to foresee it, a series of events was beginning for him, dramatic and, in part, mysterious, which were to change his life. In that period my master was living in the happy state of being in love when, in an altered perspective, you see only the best aspect of everything. He was so taken with Maria that even sexual abstinence seemed no longer to oppress him. 'You know something?' he said to me, 'even chastity has its pleasurable side. I'd forgotten that.'

She was surely the one who put certain ideas into his head: inducing him to love chastity was a way of keeping him out of the path of temptation. For that matter, their physical union was only a postponed pleasure; in the meanwhile, kisses and caresses replaced it. For Joseph, sated with excesses, restraint too was something to be savoured.

The first event was Maria's journey. One afternoon my master went to the judge's house for the official daily visit (to be repeated later and at length, unofficially, at the cistern in the garden), and he was told that Cleophas and Maria had left. At first he didn't believe it. He thought the girl was joking with him: Maria had sent the nurse to the door to give him this false news, while she watched him from some hiding-place to observe his reactions. Joseph forced himself to remain calm, and he asked to have a word with Maria's aunt.

Speaking to him from the window, Cleophas's wife begged the young man to rest assured Maria had not left by herself; the judge was with her.

So it was true.

'And here I am,' Joseph said, irked; and it was clear that he saw himself as a kind of bundle, left behind, so the travellers could move more lightly.

All right then, the girl hadn't set off alone on her journey, the way she had planned, but nevertheless she had abruptly abandoned her future husband, without a word of assent from him. If this was how their life together began, how would it continue?

Joseph was upset, distraught; his face burned with rage. He was thinking that he had made a great mistake; he had committed himself to marriage, believing that he knew Maria but, on the contrary, he didn't know her. She was not the wise, meek woman that the holy scriptures recommend as a wife; she was headstrong, unruly; she wanted to be independent. She wouldn't even be content to be her husband's equal; she would want to be his superior.

His anger was followed by dejection, because he did love Maria, and he knew she would make him suffer.

Her aunt, loyally, defended Cleophas. He had given in to Maria's pleas and decided to accompany her. That is, he kept saying no until finally he said yes. Their departure was sudden. The previous evening an opportunity had presented itself: a group of travellers, respectable people and whole families, had stopped briefly at the inn for some refreshment before resuming their journey towards Jerusalem. Cleophas and Maria joined them at the last moment. It was a spur of the moment decision; there wasn't even time to inform Joseph, as they should have done. The aunt was terribly sorry, especially since the two would be gone for perhaps three months. Besides the time of the journey, Maria was also to stay on to tend the old woman after she had given birth.

Cleophas's wife understood more than was apparent, and she felt the need to console Joseph. 'Be of good heart,' she said to him. 'When Maria makes a mistake, it is out of generosity. And besides, if she doesn't go, who will help poor Elizabeth who has no one with her, except a decrepit husband? You'll come to know her: there's no one like my Maria.'

The next day, we were working in the shop side by side, and I was keeping an eye on Joseph, because in his state of mind, he might easily have hurt himself with one of the tools; a boy came in, one Ruben, who lived near the house of Cleophas.

'From Maria,' he said, handing my master a wooden box, small but delicately worked, inlaid with ivory and gold, the work of a carver, not a carpenter. Maria had given the little coffer to the boy when she was leaving but he had forgotten to deliver it till now. Inside, when Joseph lifted the lid, he found a smooth stone with yellow veins, very like the one Maria had given him at the inn in Bethlehem and that he had later lost.

It was a message of love, tender and total, in place of a letter. Joseph clenched the stone in his hand and for a moment he and Maria were reconciled.

My master took advantage of the interruption imposed on his chaste love to make the official announcement to me and to Nathan that he was going to marry Maria, something both of us already knew quite well. He assured me that nothing in our lives would change: we would go on working there, I would live in the shed in the yard as I had done till then. We congratulated him. Nathan was happy that the child (as he called her) and the master were to marry; he had no questions, he loved them both. As for me, on the other hand, I was not at all sure that things would be the same as before. I didn't feel Nathan's unconditional love for Maria; and I knew that a woman in a house of bachelors is not exactly a blessing. To some extent she upsets you and distracts you, reminding you of things that, in her presence, it would be better to forget.

After a couple of weeks news came: Elizabeth had given birth to a son, who had been called John. Mother and child were well. It was truly a miracle: the venerable Zacharias, Elizabeth's husband, was decrepit, and the mother herself could have been not the grandmother, but the great-grandmother of the infant she had brought into the world.

More weeks went by, a month, two months; spring came and went, and a part of the summer. By now Maria had to be about to return.

She did return, in fact, one evening, almost at nightfall, but something must have happened, because she and Cleophas shut themselves up in the house and barred the doors, denying access to everyone.

The aunt tried to calm Joseph, again speaking to him from the window: it was nothing, the two travellers were just weary from their journey and wanted to rest.

Just for a moment, he begged, just one moment: to see her and greet her.

'Not now,' Maria's aunt insisted. 'They're sleeping.'

It was almost sunset: who in the world could manage to

sleep a whole night and a day? And why was there a sob in the woman's voice, and why were her eyes red from weeping?

The next day my master was told that Maria was in bed with the fever. See her? It was out of the question. He would see Cleophas then. The judge also was not well. Joseph came home unconvinced, indeed he was sure that those fevers and illnesses were hiding something. But he was far from imagining what had happened.

I knew more. Servants' gossip, rumours circulating in the market and at the taverns. It was the second, terrible blow of those that the future was keeping in store for Joseph. I didn't want to believe it but Hagar, one of the judge's maids, assured me: it was evident. Maria was pregnant.

I would more readily have accepted a blow on the head, also because I knew very well that my master was not the man responsible. To be more precise, I was dumbfounded: our Maria was incapable of any betrayal. For her to make love with a man, after her promise to Joseph, was something impossible. I had to think there had been an act of violence, a misfortune visited upon her.

This same thought was also my master's refuge, when he found out. The city's gossip didn't reach him: it was up to me to tell him.

We were working in the shop, the two of us, on the same wagon wheel. Joseph was pale, his face drawn from lack of sleep. I felt pity for him, because the world was about to crash down on him.

I said to him, in a low voice: 'Joseph, get angry.'

He looked at me, not understanding, but vaguely alarmed by my serious tone.

'Joseph, hit me.'

He still said nothing, but he put down the hammer he had been holding.

'Joseph. Maria is pregnant.'

He hit me, automatically, with his fist.

He sank to the floor, in a sitting position, pale as death. I couldn't answer all the questions he began asking me, in his agitation.

'Who was it? Tell me who it was,' he kept repeating.

'According to the family, it was you.'

'I swear before the Almighty that I didn't do it.' He held up his hand, uttering the solemn words. 'Surely Maria herself hasn't accused me,' he added. But nothing was known about what Maria was saying or not saying. At the house of Cleophas nobody was admitted.

Joseph also shut himself up in his room on the roof.

Up there, out of everyone's sight, he could give free rein to his fury, kicking the walls and asking the Lord why he was being treated in this way. He talked also with Maria: 'What did I do to you, to deserve this? Is this the way you loved me, you liar, you bitch?' His wrath against her was replaced by wrath against her still unidentified accomplice: Joseph felt a bitter relief in addressing horrible words to him, imagining that the man was in his hands and Joseph could punish him cruelly.

In the end he managed to accept the fact that she had been unfaithful to him, and again he took refuge in the thought that she must have defended herself tooth and nail, and that she had finally been overpowered. But his mind fled also from that thought, which was translated into frightful images: Maria attacked, raped, Maria screaming with no one coming to her aid.

As if trying to shake off an anguished dream, Joseph rejected those fantasies and tried in every way to elude the awareness of what had happened. He tried, that is, to think of other things; but everything brought him back to the unbearable reality: the thought of his position as promised bridegroom, the preparations that he had been making at home to receive Maria, the very room where he was now, which should have been the nuptial chamber.

He rose finally, when it was still night, and went out into the deserted streets. I followed him, because I was afraid he might do something desperate; but all he did was walk, uphill and down, throughout Nazareth. He reached the northern gate, up high, towards the hill; he came down the southern gate and the square; he crossed the city obliquely, he roamed along the walls, scowling, desperate.

Finally, towards dawn, he stopped, wheeled around, and came to me, before I could turn back or hide. He didn't ask me why I was there or why I had followed him. He sat on a doorstep, signalled me to sit beside him, and said: 'Tell me, who do you think it was? I've been turning it over in my mind all night.' He couldn't manage to persuade himself that Maria had undergone a stranger's violence.

'I've thought about it, too, but I can't think of anyone.'

We went over the list of youths and men of Nazareth, even those above suspicion, even those who couldn't have had the opportunity, a favourable occasion. But especially we reviewed the suitors, those who smiled at her during the Sabbath stroll, Hur, Joel, Tobias, Horeb, Azarias. There wasn't the slightest clue that could lead us to suspect one or the other of them. Against Hur there was his bragging, his confidence that he would marry Maria and the fact that, of all those youths, he was the one who seemed capable of violence against a woman; but there was no concrete evidence that supported an accusation.

The night paled, the light assumed that bluish transparence that heralds dawn. We heard the door of Abel the baker creak, as he is the first to open his shop, while the bread, kneaded in the evening and rising during the night, is still being baked in the oven.

'The Lord be with you, Socrates,' Joseph said to me, and he went towards home, as I walked on to buy a piece of fresh bread: the night air whets the appetite.

And so I didn't see the fight between my master and Hur. For that matter, apparently it wasn't a real fight, or even a challenge. Joseph saw the young man coming out of his house and confronted him, shaking with accumulated rage and grief. Nothing would have happened if Hur, with his usual impudence, hadn't asked him: 'Well, are you going to marry her, or do you want me to?' He was a bully and a conceited fool.

Joseph said to him grimly: 'Swear to me that you haven't spoken to her since,' and he meant since everyone had learned that he and Maria had an understanding about their betrothal.

Hur smiled, put his hand on the hilt of the dagger in his belt, and replied, looking Joseph in the face: 'And what if I had?'

At that moment Joseph released all the anger and rebellion he had been repressing within himself during those hours, and with a single blow he knocked Hur down, breaking his jaw.

I ran back, drawn by the sound of their voices. 'Help him,' Joseph said to me simply, nodding towards the braggart, who was groaning and bleeding in the street. And Joseph went on his way.

Later we found out, to my master's great dismay, that Hur couldn't have been the guilty man, because he had just come back from Schechem, where he had spent several months attending to some business matters for his father.

Understandably reserved, Joseph hadn't spoken clearly with Hur; nothing he had said would suggest that he suspected another man of having caused Maria's condition. He was actually determined to insist that he had been the one.

There was no need. All the people of the city promptly agreed that he must be responsible for what had happened. Nobody thought to consider him culpable: he was even legally in order because, after the betrothal, it was as if Maria were his wife. If anything, he was blamed for his impatience: he should have waited at least until he took her to his house after the wedding ceremony, but it was done, and that was that . . . The fact that it was the judge's niece, held up as an example of virtue, who had slipped up and committed this particular sin was a source of amusement and of endless talk. And they laughed at Cleophas, so stern and solemn, now forced to remain shut up in his house for fear of the young people's jibes and the muttering of the adults.

In other words, the city of Nazareth, unlike Joseph, didn't take it as a tragedy. The Nazarenes didn't know what he knew: that it had been someone else. My master didn't in the least care to assert the truth. Rumour gave him a role less bitter than his true one, and he accepted it. Thus he was protecting Maria's good name: the girl moved from the ranks of the unfaithful to those, less dishonourable, of over-acquiescent engaged girls.

He spent that whole day roaming around the city, as he had done during the night; but now he had a purpose, he was looking for a possible villain. He was hoping, he didn't know how, to lead one of the boys to give himself away; the guilty one, if he existed, would react when Joseph said the right words. Still, it would be a mistake to state things explicitly; Joseph would have to hint, so that only the rat he was looking for would understand.

Reasonable as it was in theory, his plan hadn't the slightest chance of success under the circumstances: lack of sleep and, even more, the weight of the torturing news that had struck him were confusing my master's mind. He walked around talking to himself, clenching his fists, and shaking his head, like a madman. He forced himself to smile, or rather to make a distorted, pathetic grimace, as he joined in the conversation of Joel, Horeb, Azarias, seeking some clue.

The provocative word, dropped casually in the midst of the talk, should suggest, he had decided, the garden of Cleophas, the most likely place where a young man of the city could lure or force Maria to sin. Anyone who involuntarily betrayed a knowledge of the place would be pointing to himself as the culprit. Now, in that garden there was an abundance of every kind of fruit and vegetable; but no melons were grown there, because the judge disliked them.

Lacking his usual wit and acumen, Joseph was clumsy when he tried to turn the subject, whatever it might be, towards gardens and produce. He would immediately find someone in the group who started bragging about his turnips or his lettuce. From turnips to melons was a logical short step, and Joseph could cast his bait. 'I have never seen,' he would say, for example, 'melons as big as the ones that grow by the cistern in the judge's garden.'

'I don't know how big Cleophas's melons are, but I'm sure mine are bigger,' someone would reply; and they would argue about the melons of Abraham and Jeremiah, and Joseph's trap would remain empty.

'Have you heard? They stole the melons from the judge's garden! The big ones, by the cistern,' my master announced, in a knot of people where Simeon the blacksmith was holding forth, a man considered sly and full of tricks. Instead of catching anybody blurting out the fact that there were no melons by the cistern, Joseph heard the smith reply: 'We all know it was you,' obviously referring to the deed everyone knew about and of which my master was innocent. He had to stifle his irritation and laugh with the others.

He gave up the idea of further traps, because the ones he thought up were no more intelligent than the first, and in his present mood he wasn't able to set them with nonchalance. He brooded on the thought of the traitor who had almost certainly possessed Maria by force but he couldn't prevent himself from thinking also of the possibility that she herself was the traitor.

She, who with him rationed her kisses and restrained his caresses to keep them from going beyond a certain point, had perhaps granted more to another man, less foolish and docile than he was. In his eyes this second hypothesis was by far the worse, making nonsense of his feelings of love. With him Maria acted shy; with the other man she abandoned her scruples. How stupid he had been, respecting her as if she were an angel, whereas she was a woman like any other, treacherous, lying.

A moment later he would repent, mentally asking Maria to forgive him for having thought such horrible things about her, and he would again be convinced that the girl had been the victim of violence and he would sympathize with her. He would imagine the scene when the criminal was about to fall on her: Maria was calling for help, crying 'Joseph', and he would arrive in time, strike down the adversary and take her, weeping, into his arms. A moment later he would be assailed by the realization that things had gone differently, and he would laugh bitterly at himself for trying, in his dreams, to forget reality.

He went through the market and he imagined that, at his appearance, from the stands and the shops there rose a murmuring, in which one word in particular stood out: 'cuckold'. The same word ran from mouth to mouth along the streets; 'cuckold' the crows cawed at him from the eastern gate, and 'cuckold' the sheep-bells repeated as the flocks returned from pasture. Until finally, as he passed the tavern, he really did hear that word, fired like a bullet, and it seemed to be coming from the door, aimed at him. He went inside like a cyclone, furious. 'Who was it?' he yelled.

'Who was it who did what?' they asked him, bewildered.

'Nothing, nothing,' Joseph said, regaining his self-control. He turned and left.

Later, running into Joel who was going about his business, Joseph detained him with pointless, rambling talk; the boy thought Joseph was trying to start something.

'You want us to have another fight?' Joel asked him, annoyed.

'Me? The thought never crossed my mind.'

'Then what do you want from me, Joseph son of Jacob?'

'I'd like you to tell me something,' my master said, heatedly.

'What's that?'

After thinking a moment, Joseph answered, 'Nothing.'

'What do you mean, nothing? Tell me. Don't be afraid.'

'Nothing,' my master repeated. He went off shaking his head, repeating his word, nothing, like some ritual formula.

At the end of that day, which for him was very long, he found himself circling the house of Cleophas. He walked through the garden, as far as the cistern, but as he had foreseen, Maria wasn't there. She hadn't waited for him at her window, looking down; she hadn't come to him, to confess finally the truth. He would have liked to confront her, to learn from her what had happened. To know the exact extent of his own misfortune, to find out if he had been betrayed or not, to confirm for himself that Maria had been forced into it, that she had defended herself, had screamed and wept, would have alleviated his suffering.

He went then up to the house and he saw her at last, in profile, in the rectangle of the window: she had remained spellbound by some thought as she was sewing, and she was smiling. She didn't seem distressed or tormented, as he would have expected to find her; she seemed to him more beautiful, but suddenly more incomprehensible. He was seething with rage and shame, and there she was smiling.

Cleophas knew that it hadn't been Joseph. Maria had sworn this to her uncle, and he believed her. But the girl refused to say who was responsible then and later.

There was only one thing left to do for a just man: Cleophas hesitated a long time, then he went to Joseph. He turned up at the shop one afternoon, stiff as a pole; he greeted my master, invoking the Almighty's blessing on him, and announced that he had come to speak of serious and delicate matters. Nathan and I went out, but we didn't fail to eavesdrop. The judge in the carpenter's shop: this was an event.

'Forgive me,' Cleophas said. 'I thought it was you.' Then he produced the five silver shekels that Joseph had paid him to have Maria in marriage; the judge meant to return them. Joseph waved the money away.

'You can reputidate her; that is your right,' Cleophas declared, to explain the meaning of his gesture. And, in fact, returning money without being asked in this country is unusual behaviour, which demands explanation.

Cleophas humbled himself before my master, who was just as embarrassed as the older man, if not more so. Joseph was somewhat pleased that his innocence was recognized, but he was not prepared to inveigh against Maria. Repudiate her, her uncle said, you have the right. But what did he, Cleophas, know about what really happened? If this is how justice is meted out in Israel, without compassion, then who is safe?

The judge, having rid himself of a burden, began to talk, to tell; but he knew nothing about the original deed; he knew only the consequences. Apparently nobody knew (as Joseph discovered by his questioning), not the judge, not his wife, not the maidservants of the house, how the thing could have happened. Maria had never gone out alone; she spoke with no one. It would seem, as Cleophas put it, that the girl's condition were the work of some spirit.

Even during the journey nothing had happened, no incident of any kind. Maria slept in inns on two nights, in the same room with the wife of a landowner, an elderly woman and a light sleeper. In Elizabeth's house the girl was never alone, she never went off, not even after the child's birth, not even to go down to the fountain at the crossroads, a stone's throw from the courtyard. And she had been so alert and sensitive in assisting her aunt, prudent even in her inexperience and ready to accept the animal reality of procreation, as if she had always helped mothers give birth.

'You should have seen old Zacharias, how moved he was,' the judge recalled, 'on seeing a son. He wept, nearly blind as he is, and he raised his hands to heaven.'

Then he began talking again about Maria: 'She did put on a little weight . . . I would have expected her, on the contrary, to waste away. She often had to get up at night because Elizabeth had no milk and Maria would warm some goat's milk for the baby. By then it was obvious that the girl's belly was swelling, but fortunately neither Zacharias nor Elizabeth noticed. I hadn't paid any attention to it myself, I was so far from imagining that such a thing could happen.'

During the return journey Maria's condition could no longer be concealed. Cleophas, who had finally realized it but was unwilling to believe it, was forced to accept the reality of it by an inn-keeper's words.

'He gave her the best room,' Cleophas told Joseph, 'saying

that my wife, in her condition, needed care. A kind man. But it was as if he had stabbed me with a dagger.'

Then there was a scene with Maria, who admitted that she was with child, but would say no more than that.

The two didn't speak again; or rather, Cleophas wouldn't say another word to his niece, until finally, after they were home, she confronted him, but only to insist that it hadn't been Joseph.

My master was pursuing a certain train of thought: if what Cleophas said was true, the thing must have happened before their departure. Maria was guarded also in Nazareth, kept in the house, accompanied by someone the few times she went out; but he himself knew from experience that a bold man could have found a way to meet her in secret.

His suspicions about her were rekindled: she must have at least offered her seducer some opportunity. Joseph was grateful to her, all the same, for the straightforward way she exculpated him to her relatives.

Cleophas remained seated in the shop for a long time; perhaps he found some solace in the company of the betrayed bridegroom who did not moan or utter recriminations and who, whatever he said about Maria, did not condemn her. The judge muttered, cleared his throat; he felt that here his dignity was not threatened, and so he abandoned the stiffness he had imposed on himself. Indeed, he bent over, leaning on his stick, assuming the attitude of an old man.

'Who would ever have said . . . at my age . . . that pure, innocent child . . . but then . . . How can it have happened? I don't understand it, may the Lord help me.'

After having repeated these and other, similar words over and over, Cleophas stood up, called the Almighty's blessing on Joseph once again, unsure whether he should consider my master his future nephew-in-law or not, but sure that Joseph was an upright man, worthy of friendship and patronage; and he left.

Unable to work any more, Joseph climbed up to the roof, actually on to the roof of the upper room, the place where he sought refuge those days, to ponder his uncertainty. He didn't so much ponder as chew it over, actually grinding his teeth. Who can it have been? And, first of all, what really happened? Should he repudiate Maria? She was refusing to see him. Why?

From up there he could see the city below him, its streets, the synagogue; he recognized the tavern, the shops, the market, the washing-place, the houses where the young men of the Sabbath stroll lived. He followed everyone's movements, in search of something, though he himself didn't know what: something that would indicate the guilty man to him. Suddenly, inspired by some suspicion or intuition, he came down and went roaming through the streets, closed in himself, concentrating, because it was supremely important that his investigation remain secret. He listened to the women's talk in the market, the drunks in the tavern, in case he might catch a revelatory word.

At the same time he was paying heed to thoughts of another kind: a word from him and his commitment to Maria would be ended. Cleophas himself recognized Joseph's right to repudiate her. The nightmare of marriage would no longer haunt him; he would return to his former, carefree liberty.

But then, in his memory, he saw the face, the form of Maria; he heard again the words of love she had spoken to him; he could almost feel her kisses on his lips, smell her perfume in his nostrils, as the suffering of betrayal and abandonment created turmoil in his spirit.

He always ended up going back to the garden of Cleophas, hiding among the broad beans and the onions. Lying on the ground, he would eat a green pepper, to sharpen the bitterness in his mouth. Maria didn't show herself. Perhaps she was afraid of him, or ashamed.

One evening he went out into the fields, gathered a great bunch of wild flowers, crocus and narcissus, dog roses and red anemomes, bound them together, surrounding them with laurel leaves, and took them to Maria. He hung the nosegay at her window, when it was already dark and the family had gathered for supper.

In a contradiction that was only too apparent, he turned the axe-handle, signalling to Dorothea to come. When it was dark, the Greek woman slipped through the gap in the wall. Joseph was still awake, seated on the roof. He joined her in the yard.

'How are you?' she asked, replying to his greeting. 'I heard what happened to you, and I'm sorry. Can I be of help in any way? Perhaps you could tell me everything, get it off your chest: that's what friends are for.'

In the swaying beam of the lantern, which Joseph had lighted, her veil, worked with gold threads, shimmered; her white leg gleamed, emerging from a split in her Greek dress, and her sandal of tender hyena hide revealed her restless foot.

'Aren't you going to invite me inside?' Dorothea asked. 'We'll talk for a moment, and then I'll go.'

Joseph followed her into the shed, shifted the beam, sat down with her on the bed. Playing her role, she offered him the consolations of Stoic philosophy, very much in fashion in Athens and Rome then; and as she spoke, she removed her veil, and let her dress slip over her shoulders. Joseph saw again the beautiful bosom, which he thought he had renounced forever; he smelled the unmistakable perfume that so aroused him. He could have left; there was still time. Long abstinence and the tension of his nerves created in him a frenzy never felt before, and he flung himself on Dorothea as if plunging into the abyss.

X

Late that night, he again walked the breadth of Cleophas's garden and, when he came to the house, he climbed up the wall. He thrust his feet into the cracks in the plaster and managed to grasp the bars of Maria's window.

Dorothea's embraces earlier in the evening had been neither a surrogate nor a remedy of love, but simply a lapse into profanity, into the man that Joseph had been before falling in love. He regretted them, but he also felt justified. He had not been the first to break the promise of fidelity. He dismissed from his mind the vulgar idea of paying back Maria's betrayal, and he was mostly sorry that he hadn't resisted temptation.'

Now he had to repeat to himself his good intentions, then think of it no more. It was pointless to feel guilty, recriminations were futile. Precisely because with the Greek woman he had given way, he should understand all the better Maria's bewilderment, and consider that she might have succumbed to a similar temptation. But all his background drove him to believe that women had a different role from men, with stricter obligations and narrower confines of independence. She had sinned, she was guilty; and she was guilty even if she had undergone violence, because she had given a man other than Joseph the opportunity to approach her.

So he looked in at the window in the mood of a man who is coming to ask for an accounting, supported by the law, and by custom, with justifiable impatience, heedless of the time and the place. But naturally he wasn't all that sure of himself because, even if she had betrayed him, he still loved her.

Maria came to the window, greeted him as if she had left him the day before and nothing had happened in the meanwhile.

'Tell me just one thing,' he began, 'Did you have to submit to violence?'

She answered no.

'Were you forced in any way?'

Maria, again, said no.

Gripping the bars of the window with his left hand and waving his right as if to fan the fever of his speech, Joseph went on: 'Then why have you done this to me? Don't you remember that you promised yourself to me, and we kissed, down there, at the cistern? Is your word worth so little? . . . ' And he continued reproaching her for her faithlessness and, while he was about it, for her sudden departure which he had forbidden, and which, in his opinion, was the origin of all this misfortune. What was she punishing him for? Hadn't she given any thought to him? Did she have any idea of the terrible time he was having now? And he ended with the question that had been tormenting him ever since he first heard the news: 'Who was it? Tell me, who was it?'

Maria didn't answer. In the end, as Joseph wouldn't stop pressing her, she said to him: 'If you really love me, you must never ask me anything.'

And she wouldn't be budged then. This was the third misfortune that befell my master: Maria's reticence. Insist as he might, the girl kept stubbornly silent. Giving up the idea of knowing the man's name to Joseph seemed almost more unbearable than the betrayal in itself: vengeance was his dominating thought at that moment.

With that rapidity the mind often displays in adjusting to a changed situation, Joseph immediately saw the deed in a new perspective. It was obvious that Maria wanted to shield someone, and surely not some boy of twenty like those who strolled around the square on the sabbath. It had to be some person of authority who would be socially destroyed by the revelation, a Levite, a scribe, a Pharisee, a doctor of the law. Or else a magistrate: for a moment Joseph thought of Cleophas, then smiled at his own thoughts.

'It's dark here,' he said, 'let's go down to the cistern.'

Maria hadn't dared light the lamp. In the shadowy room Joseph couldn't see her distinctly. There was something changed in her, or so it seemed to him: a new composure, a pensive manner, which intimidated him at times.

A huge, round moon flooded the garden with patches of white light and made the shadows deeper. She had covered her head with a shawl. She hadn't aged in those months, Joseph said to himself, but she had become an adult. She seemed reserved to him, serious, and very sweet.

He took her hands. 'At least explain why you don't want to tell me . . . '

'You wouldn't understand,' Maria answered. 'It's not a secret, but it's something I can't tell . . . something you could never believe. If you love me, leave it at that. The only thing I can tell you is . . . that I love you, I have never stopped loving you, not even for a moment.'

'But if that's so then – ' Joseph began.

She interrupted him. 'I said before: if you never ask me anything, then I'll know that you love me, too.'

Joseph pondered her demand, which seemed to him not only unbearable but also illogical. 'Your uncle says I should repudiate you,' he murmured finally, concluding his own, unspoken line of reasoning.

'My uncle . . . ' Maria said. 'And what about you?'

Joseph didn't speak. 'I love you,' he murmured, simply.

That, in the end, was the real confession, which did not justify Maria's guilt, but erased it, and it reflected my master's great, tormenting desire to believe her. Tormenting, because he loved logic as much as a Greek would (and that love of his for logic had grown stronger while he lived with me), and Maria offered him only an invitation to close his eyes and entrust himself to his feelings.

She held out her arms to him; he clasped her furiously to his chest and really did close his eyes. In a clear, profound voice Maria said to him: 'I haven't betrayed you,' and Joseph renounced the logic of the Greeks in order to accept the reasoning of love. He knew that Maria always told the truth, and therefore, incredible as it might seem, what she had declared must be true. He kissed her wildly; then, respecting the restraint and modesty with which she responded to him, he began kissing her more gently, stroking here face and her hair. Her shawl had dropped to the ground; in the moonlight, Maria was close, shy, and at the same time remote, enveloped in a halo of light. She was crying.

Those tears convinced Joseph that the girl, probably during the journey, had been the victim of violence, outrageous and sudden, from a stranger, a bandit, a soldier, in any case a foreigner. She had been overwhelmed by it, and couldn't bear talking about it. He understood her shamed privacy, the offence to her modesty; and he was silent.

Joseph vowed to himself that he would never speak to her again about the thing that had come between them, and for a long time he stuck to his intention: a sense of modesty prevented him from making the slightest hint in her presence. He was prepared to consider the boy (or girl) that was to be born as his own child, no longer investigating the mystery of its paternity.

One morning, with the attitude of a resolute and happy future husband, Joseph spoke to me and Nathan, announcing that he was going to be married.

I should have kept my mouth shut, but instead I asked him: 'Have you forgiven Maria?'

'There was no need,' he answered; he told us that she had been subjected to violence and therefore had to ask no one's forgiveness. He said that an angel had appeared to him in a dream, assuring him that Maria was blameless and had told him to receive her into his house without fear.

The children of Israel are suspicious also when it comes to dreams, but when an angel appears to you, then the dream becomes a revelation, a message from the Almighty, and you believe in it as you believe in the commandments. I wasn't sure, however, that Joseph had dreamed of an angel because, unlike Maria, he didn't always tell the truth; it occurred to me that he might be using this means to justify to us his decision to marry. In Nazareth only the two of us, Nathan and I (not counting Cleophas), knew that Joseph hadn't been the one to get her with child. We were friends, employees, but also judges of his actions.

The day after his night-time meeting with Maria my master began to be received again in the house of Cleophas, and he also resumed seeing the girl by the cistern at sunset. I wasn't interested in knowing what they said to each other, convinced that lovers' talk is always the same and I was wrong, because it is unlikely that they reached an agreement about certain aspects of their future behaviour.

I should have suspected that everything wasn't going so smoothly between the pair, because Joseph was more nervous than ever and so sunk in his thoughts that you had to call him three times before he would listen to you. These distractions also, in my view, were one aspect of his anxiety over the imminent marriage, and I didn't think they were anything to worry about. With only two weeks to go, we were all involved in the preparations of the wedding feast, to which, as custom required, all citizens would be invited; so I couldn't waste any time speculating on his moods!

Only a couple of days before the ceremony Joseph calmed down. He was serene, joking with us as he used to. I was concerned because he wasn't bothering about the things that usually keep the bridegroom and host anxious: the tables, the benches, the garlands, the wine. I'll tell you the truth: he behaved like an adult taking part in a children's game.

I still hadn't realized how beautiful Maria was. When she was brought to the bridegroom's house, on the eve of the wedding, reclining in a palanquin, her hair loose below her veil, the gold pieces touching her brow, we looked at her, all of us, as if we didn't know her. Her dress outlined her figure, and I saw that her body was as graceful as Dorothea's. Maria's face was truly fascinating: charged with a vigorous, earthly beauty, red lips, black eyes and hair, but all glowing with a light that refined her. Maria didn't arouse in me, as I had feared, any bad thoughts.

She was light-hearted, she responded to the traditional pranks. She joked with Joseph, who had come out to greet the little procession and welcome her. 'Who is this man, redolent of incense and myrrh, and of all the spices that the caravans bring to Israel? Why did I not see him before the man who is to be my husband?'

Joseph bent over her and said: 'How beautiful you are, my beloved, my dove who hides in the cleft of the rock!'

Everyone applauded, and Uncle Cleophas blessed the couple.

The actual ceremony took place the following day. I took charge of everything, because once Maria had arrived Joseph was completely helpless. I divided the supper guests, separating the men from the women; I also divided the betrothed couple, sending Maria to sleep with her girlfriends, while Joseph presided over the table, accepting everyone's congratulations, taking part in the fun and the dancing.

The next day all went well. The yard filled with people during the morning; the young men challenged each other to race or jump, or else they tried to climb a pole smeared with sheep grease, to snatch the silver piece glued to the top. Towards evening, when the tables were ready, the bridegroom came downstairs. The maidens lighted his way with burning lamps.

Maria was seated under the bridal canopy. She was stirred from her smiling gravity only when Joseph was led before her by ten of the beautiful girls in the festive dress. He seemed awkward.

'Come,' she said to him, 'you have to marry only one girl: me. I saw you first.' She was seized by a great desire to laugh, and she couldn't manage to contain herself. Infected, Joseph laughed, too; every time he tried to stop, he would look at Maria's laughing face and would start all over again. The girls joined in, releasing an urge that had been tickling them for hours, behind their composure. Soon everyone was laughing, including me. It was an unheard of scandal, but nobody cared.

Drying the tears his hearty laughter had caused (for he too had joined in, though he couldn't say why), Cleophas scattered a handful of wheat and broke a jar of nard, whose penetrating odour filled the house and the courtyard. Once these fertility rites had been performed, the crowd ate and drank with such gusto that ten serving boys and the same number of old women couldn't keep the tables supplied.

Joseph and Maria, now his wife, had gone up to the room on the roof once the meal had got underway. I didn't know which way to turn, trying to deal with everything, but I stole a moment to climb up to the roof myself, by the outside stairs, to see if the couple needed anything. From the bedroom a murmuring came, a liquid and whispering sound: it was Maria, and I couldn't tell whether she was laughing or crying. I was reassured when I heard Joseph's voice, as he said distinctly: 'What do you mean, there's no difference? We've never been alone, together, in the same room . . . '

'That time you climbed up from the garden, at night . . . '

'That doesn't count. You were inside and I was outside, hanging on to the bars . . . '

' . . . and there was no telling which of us was in prison: you glued to the bars or me, who hadn't left the house for two weeks . . . ' and Maria began to laugh again, and Joseph did the same. I went downstairs immediately: they didn't need anything.

The wedding feast lasted seven days. Every evening the bridal couple joined the guests to eat and drink, dance and sing. Then we shut the gate, sent everyone home, and Joseph and Maria were finally alone.

In the early days of their marriage it seemed that the two of them had forgotten the unfortunate event and that Maria's pregnancy, now in the fifth month, was the normal result of love between a husband and a wife. She, more than Joseph, took care to act as if nothing had happened. I'm sure that at times she really did forget.

I would see her laugh at the slightest excuse, often it seemed for no reason at all, as on the wedding day. Nathan followed her around, like a dog following his master. He had made a puppet for her, with a wooden head; the puppet would stick his tongue out, and Maria would laugh. Unable to make the puppet speak, Nathan would grunt for it, and again Maria would laugh.

Joseph chased her in the yard, pretending he wanted to catch her; she ran till she was out of breath and then, gasping, she would give up, taking refuge in the arms of her pursuer. 'If you can't have pity on me, sir,' she said, 'have some compassion for the child I am carrying in my womb.'

Then she stopped laughing: suddenly her words seemed beyond the game, deeply serious. Joseph looked at her, shaking his head, reassuring her with a caress, a kiss.

Maria worked with the steady shrewdness of a mature woman. She ground the wheat, baked the bread, fetched water from the well. She washed the clothes, swept and dusted, cooked, set the olives on the table, and the fruit, the bean soup, the roast lamb or the fish, the greens, the cake of honey and almonds. She served Joseph, then carried our share to Nathan and me, in the shop.

She ate standing up, like other women in her position. Behaving unusually for a man, Joseph insisted she sit down at the table. Maria demurred. Until, for a certain period, he also ate standing up.

Nathan and I, tacitly, lent her a hand, relieving her of the hardest tasks: we filled all the vessels in the house with water; we ground a bushel of wheat between two stones. She looked after us, saw to it that we were well fed, that my sheets were fresh and clean.

To Joseph she showed all those little attentions, that tender concern that her love for him prompted. From time to time she would play some little joke on him. Joseph would pick out a raw egg to suck, hold it to his lips; but nothing came. She laughed to see her husband's face, his amazed look, as if offended that one of the hens had laid an empty shell instead of an egg. Joseph then realized that she had been the one to pierce the egg and drain it, as a little surprise for him; and he then laughed, too.

On other occasions Maria received the surprise. She would take the baby chicks their mash and, among all the pretty little animals, one would come prancing forward, a deep purple. She, too, would for a moment think of some miracle, then would realize that Joseph had painted the chick. And, laughing, she would chase her husband.

As I think back now, I see that their behaviour was hiding something. Not that their love was a pretence, an act, because their love transpired from every gesture, every word, in all its reality. But it was certaintly different from the love of other couples, other marriages that I had known. One moment they were very serious, each in his own thoughts; a little later they would give way to an explosion of merriment, nervous, without reason. They laughed for the sheer pleasure of laughing, like children. Their hilarity was contagious, precisely because of its innocence. I saw them exchange a caress, a kiss, with care to keep their act within certain limits, to restrain it. I thought they didn't want to force us to witness their effusions, out of respect for themselves and for others.

Joseph from time to time had to be absent for a whole day, sometimes two, when he went up into the hills to buy logs, of oak, or sycamore, cedar, walnut; or to deliver some finished piece of work, a wagon, a yoke, a plough, or bins, cupboards, to customers of ours who lived in the country. It was as if he were going off to war: Maria would cling to him, repeating – though she knew it was useless – her request to go with him. She would give him sacks with food she had prepared, bread and wine in one, and in the other a piece of roast kid, olives, dates, honey cakes. Joseph would get on to the wagon, with the mules he had hired from Joel's father, crack the whip, and leave.

Once when he was going on such an expedition after his marriage, he stopped when he was just outside the city. He heard a sound of knocking from inside a chest that was a part of his load. He raised the lid, and inside was Maria, who sat up, gasping for breath. She had hidden there after saying goodbye to her husband, exploiting the moment when he was climbing on to the box, with his back to her, and thus accompanying him secretly. But then she was about to suffocate. 'I'll take you home,' Joseph said, turning the mules around. He smiled at her, more flattered than annoyed.

'I'll take you.' Maria seized the reins and drove to our yard, where, after a complete turn, she stopped the wagon at the gate, ready to set off again. I don't know who had taught her, but she drove very well.

On his return Joseph brought her presents: not city products, not jewels or chased articles, because there was nothing like that where he went; but flowers, red anemones, lilies, wild tulips, hyacinths, narcissus, or a bird in a cage, a pair of doves. Maria would run out into the street to welcome him, at the risk of being knocked down by the mules.

There was no money in the house, because Joseph's savings had been consumed by the wedding-feast; but Maria was such a good manager that, little by little, the new family accumulated an emergency fund. Seated on the tiny chair that used to be reserved for her, when she came to visit our shop every day, Maria prepared things for the child, little shirts, swaddling clothes. Next to her Joseph planed the planks for the cradle, fitted them together, inlaid the sides.

'It's too beautiful,' Maria said to him one day.

'Nothing is too beautiful for your son,' he answered. He saw her eyes cloud over, swollen with tears; Maria had sensed something in those words that excluded Joseph from the role of parent. 'For our son,' he added, correcting himself, and Maria smiled at him.

One evening I was sitting in the yard with them after supper: we usually lingered there long enough for Joseph to organize the next day's work with me, then we would separate, I would retire to my shed, and they would climb to the upper room.

Maria talked always about the baby, describing him as if he

already existed, what he would be like at the age of six, or ten, or twenty.

'I understand,' I said, laughing, 'he's going to be the most beautiful child in the world.'

'No,' Maria replied, seriously, 'he'll be the most important child in the world.'

Her words struck me, not so much because of their literal meaning but because of the confidence with which she had uttered them. It's normal for mothers to dream that their children will have what they themselves never had. Maria had always made it clear that she felt called to fulfil some exceptional destiny, and here she was married to a carpenter without ambitions. It was understandable that she thought her son would compensate. She was sure her child would be a boy.

I looked at Joseph and I saw that those words, on the contrary, had reminded him of a nagging thought: he had sensed some reference to the importance of the child's father, the real father.

And so, involuntarily, they wounded each other. One word was enough to make Joseph's old torment begin again: he couldn't then dispel from his mind the thought of the other man, and the questions Maria had left without answers.

But in Nazareth what eminent man was there, whose great dignity would be reflected on his son? To hear Maria talk, you would think she was carrying a king's son in her womb; but the father could also be a rich man, a religious figure, a man of moral authority, or even someone whose social rank was barely higher than Joseph's but who, in the benighted provinces, seemed a figure of great prominence.

My master went back to roaming the streets; for long stretches he would follow the most different sort of people, the teacher of the synagogue, Esau the scribe, Habinadab the judge, a younger colleague of Cleophas, a brilliant man with a great political career ahead of him. In this way he discovered a number of things about the private lives of our most distinguished fellow citizens, but nothing that could enlighten him about the one question that interested him.

In the evening he would go out, to the tavern. Like many other wives in Nazareth, Maria stayed at home and waited for her husband. She turned out the lamp to save oil, and in the darkness her thoughts would also turn dark. She had hoped that Joseph was different, that he wouldn't assign her a role she loathed, only a few weeks after the wedding: the role of stupid and faithful wife, good only for waiting and obeying. She realized, all the same, that her husband had his reasons for behaving like this.

Wine, for Joseph, had become a sedative: it dissolved his anguish, it separated him from reality. Sometimes when he drank, he went too far and slumped in one corner of the tavern, drunk. Respectfully, people pretended not to see him. When it grew very late, Maria would come and knock at my shed; Joseph still hadn't come home. I knew where to go and look for him. I helped set him on his feet again and dragged him home.

One night when he was drunker than usual, my master slipped from my grasp and fell, on his behind, in the middle of the street. It was a bright moonlight night, you could see as clearly as if it were day. The houses, in that light, looked different; as if they were not made of stone but of painted canvas.

With the rhetorical emphasis that drunks sometimes muster, Joseph began an invective against the people of Nazareth: 'May thunderbolts fall upon your heads, citizens of this city, who are harbouring a traitor in your midst. May your houses fall down, may your walls be levelled, and salt sown over the ruins . . . '

After preaching in this way for a long time, he lowered his voice and spoke to himself, not so much with sympathy as with anger: 'Look at the man I've become,' he said, 'a cuckold before I was a bridegroom. I! Who could have had my choice of all the virgins of this city. And she doesn't say a thing. She won't talk, won't tell who it was.' He was referring to Maria. When he was in that condition, he never uttered her name. 'One of these nights I'll get really drunk, I'll go home, and I'll force that name out of her, one way or another.'

His words were incoherent, stammered out, but that was what he was saying.

'Hadn't you decided not to think about it any more?' I reminded him.

'Not think about it, you say. How can I help it?' He looked at me with furious, tearful eyes. 'You still don't know the whole thing . . . ' And he burst out laughing.

'Maria's faithful to you now.'

He laughed again, heartily as if in what I had said there was god knows what hidden source of hilarity. Then he winked, half-sly, half-desolate, and went on: 'Faithful? Not to me, brother, not to me . . . '

I didn't bother to try to find any meaning in his words; they were just the ravings of a drunk. I lifted him from the ground and we went on our way homewards.

As if to make amends for the accusations he had hurled at her, my master began a whining eulogy of his wife: Maria was good, hard-working, a fine cook; she showed every consideration for him; he would cut off his hand rather than raise it against her.

Meanwhile we had come to the yard. Maria lighted the lamp. 'You see?' Joseph said. 'She's waiting for me?' He stumbled over the threshold, and she held him, leading him to a chair. He couldn't keep his head erect; it slumped on his chest. Maria stroked his hair, dried his sweat with a cloth.

Then my master spoke as if he were perfectly sober: 'What does the past matter?' he said. 'What's past is past. If we love each other in the present, let's forget all the rest.' His drunken state was revealed in the words that followed, which he would never have uttered with a clear mind. 'What do I care?' he went on, 'Even if I never find out the name of that dog who made you pregnant?'

Maria sprang to her feet, insulted, I believe, by the vulgar words that had escaped her husband's lips. She was trembling. She knelt down and said a prayer in praise of the Almighty. Joseph paid no attention: he had fallen asleep, with his head on the table.

Jealousy, in those days, destroyed my master like a disease: it poisoned his every pleasure, stole into his every thought. Maria said nothing; on the contrary, she tried bravely to keep up, in front of Nathan and me, a semblance of good humour, as if things between her and her husband were going perfectly.

Joseph studied every act of hers, every expression, trying to catch her off guard and read who knows what in her face. Recovering himself after those moments of suspicion, he would feel shame. He would clasp her to him in a corner of the ground-floor room or behind the well in the yard, where he thought they were unseen: a furious, silent embrace. Then he would let go of her, without kissing her.

What was my master jealous of? I asked myself that question, because Maria's behaviour was beyond reproach. In my view, he suffered a kind of intermittent fever; when his rages passed, the very presence of his wife, serene and smiling, would calm him. It seemed to him impossible to suspect Maria, while she was smiling at him.

The moment Joseph was away from the house, the suspicious working of his mind would begin again. One day he set off, as he regularly did from time to time, with the wagon and mules towards the mountain to collect a load of logs, but instead of admiring the landscape (which was worth admiration), he brooded on a series of imaginary scenes that enraged him. The mules knew the way and proceeded without being driven, so Joseph could indulge in his tormented fantasies.

In his mind he saw a man cross our yard at night, then climb the outside stairs to the upper room, where Maria was sleeping. The man was well-dressed, a figure of authority, middle-aged, blond, with pale eyes, a physical type not usually found in Israel. Joseph imagined him as someone different, a foreigner, as if to reassure himself that it was someone unknown to him, like one of the barbarians from the north who served in the Roman army.

The man, who in Joseph's sick imagination was the baby's real father, was blackmailing Maria, forcing her to receive him when her husband was absent. Joseph was forgetting that I am a light sleeper and nobody could enter our yard at night without my being aware of it.

My master that morning stopped the wagon and, making a sudden decision, turned into a side road and then into the barnyard of a farm he knew. He hadn't gone far from Nazareth and could return on foot. He had covered perhaps a stadium of the way home when he felt ashamed of himself: he went back and recovered the wagon.

But when he reached the yard of the farm, he recalled that other yard, his own, and he was stung by a searing curiosity to see what Maria did when he wasn't there. He went to the road again and came home. He slipped into the woodshed, the same hiding-place where he had formerly welcomed Dorothea. He spent the night hours watching, listening for a footstep on the gravel, peering through the cracks to see the shadow of a cloaked man heading for the house. The only shadow that crossed the yard was his own: starving, on the second night Joseph slipped from his lair and went to steal some of his own bread from the bin.

I caught him as he was coming back, trying to slip into his hiding-place. It was the dead of night.

'Shouldn't you be on Mount Carmel, loading wood?' I asked him.

'I am on Mount Carmel and I am loading wood,' he answered at me, winking. Dirty, his hair sticking to his brow, he looked like a madman.

I brought him some more food and a jug of water.

'What are you hoping to see?'

'Nothing,' he said. 'What I really want to see is nothing, and nobody.'

Really this was exactly what Joseph wanted: to be sure that nothing happened, that nobody ventured into the yard at night.

He called me back when I was about to leave him. 'You'll think I'm a madman,' he said to me. 'Think that if you want, but don't tell her I was here.'

'I'm too fond of her,' I answered, 'to sadden her with your suspicions. You should know me.'

'You're right,' he admitted, and he asked my forgiveness.

He set off again early that morning, to go and collect the wagon. God knows what he had thought he would find, as a night-time visitor to our yard. I felt sorry for him, but when I thought of him keeping watch for two nights in that hole, still impregnated with Dorothea's perfume, he who had never had any opportunity to be jealous, I had to laugh.

He came back that same day, towards evening, saying he hadn't found the wood he wanted. He brought Maria an ankle bracelet, of gold, as a present. He had bought it somewhere or other. Splendidly worked, it had cost him almost the whole sum he had set aside to buy us a supply of wood.

Maria kissed his hand as a sign of gratitude. She scolded him affectionately for having spent so much money on her, but she was pleased. She tried on the bracelet at once; it fitted her slim ankle perfectly, and all the next day she wore the ornament around the house. She constantly looked down at her foot and made the jewel glint in the sunlight. Knowing she had that gold there, around her ankle, made the bracelet heavier than it truly was; she walked slowly, with a different step. She showed it off to Nathan and me, naturally; then she stood at the gate, leaning on the post with studied indifference, so that the occasional passer-by could also admire the jewel.

Seeing her child-like enthusiasm, Joseph had to ask himself: how was it possible for her to wrong me? How can she have been in another man's arms? She had said to him: 'I haven't betrayed you,' and it was true that Maria never told lies. How many times had he tried to make sense of those words! How often had he pondered them and studied them, trying to dismiss the brutal reality of her union with another man. But Maria was pregnant, and what Joseph wanted was, finally, an impossible thing, a denial of the laws of nature.

He forgot everything the moment she put her hand in his, smiling as always. Maria had got into the habit of taking a stroll at evening, holding him by the hand, all around the yard. They talked of the little events of the day, they looked at the sky and the trees, as they changed colour. She felt her heart gripped as darkness came, and she would huddle in Joseph's arms. He would hold her in a tight embrace.

Joseph wasn't the only one to suffer an attack of jealousy. It also happened to Maria.

One evening the little family had barely sat down at table when Jacob the coppersmith and his wife turned up at the shop. He owed us two silver shekels for various pieces of furniture we had made for him. Joseph stood up and went into the other room to receive him.

The veiled woman, accompanying her husband and standing a few paces away from him, uncovered her face; she was Daniel's Maria, the girl who several years earlier had falsely accused Joseph before the council of elders of having violated her among the bushes of the yard. The coppersmith, dark and lame, was the only man in the city who would have her as a wife, because even then Maria had been known as a woman of easy ways, generous with her body.

She was large, pale; her face was painted with care and, as always, she had done her hair well. She was dressed like a lady, breathing strong perfumes. She had been ruined by the malicious chatter of her girlfriends and their mothers. The girl had hoped that, once she was married, the gossips would calm down. But on the contrary, she still bore the reputation of being a woman who readily granted her favours to men. When she had seen it was pointless to try to change people's opinion of her, Maria had decided to act on it. They had accused her for a single mistake (or perhaps a couple) committed in girlhood. Well, she would give them material for a dozen accusations, with some basis in fact. So they said she was a provocative girl? Well, she would be worse: a seductress.

Joseph recognized her at once and blushed. He knew all about her, even that one day they had dragged her beneath the walls with the intention of stoning her, then and there, without accusing witnesses, without a trial. She had stood there, her legs parted, looking at the people, fearlessly.

'You want to punish me,' she said then, 'according to the Law. Very well. But the Law prescribes that the man who has sinned with me should undergo the same punishment.' She looked around, as if to choose among her persecutors the man she would accuse first. 'I see more than one here,' she continued, 'who has committed adultery in my bed. I am thinking that they should join me now. What about you, Isaiah? Do you want to come? You who accuse your wife of having foul breath? Or you, Judah, son of Zebedee, who still hide and wait for me in the narrow streets? Or you, Ruben, son of Benjamin, who came to me with a full purse and I rejected your money, because I either sin for nothing or I don't sin? But I didn't send you away. You begged me on your knees and kissed the hem of my dress . . . '

There was no telling how long the woman would have gone on, but the crowd of listeners was thinning, and in the end there was no one left. Daniel's Maria saw only the bent backs of husbands hurrying away and of scowling wives chasing them. After that she was considered a disciple of Lucifer, and she was surely the most beautiful of fallen angels. Her husband knew and kept silent; indeed, with her he was deaf and blind, just to be able to stay with her.

Aware of Maria's reputation, my master felt ill-at-ease. The woman gazed at him shamelessly; she didn't say a word to him, but those glances and her languid, lascivious manner were a signal that anyone would have understood.

As if by chance, Maria, our own Maria, came into the shop

from the next room, looked the other woman up and down, without speaking, then apologized for having interrupted the conversation between the two men. She had easily recognized the woman and had observed Joseph's embarrassment. When supper was resumed, both he and she avoided mentioning the matter.

The next day Daniel's Maria waited for my master outside the wall of the yard, hidden among the bushes, now very high, that spilled over to the street. Joseph heard a low voice and he looked over the wall: the temptress was there, fresh and scented; the sun danced on her tunic and on her hair.

'Joseph,' she said to him. 'You remember how much in love with you I was, all those years ago? I was ready to do anything in order to marry you. You didn't want me, and because of your rejection I've become what I am . . . but my heart is still yours. What am I to do?'

He foolishly replied as if she really had asked him for advice; he recommended that she drive away all temptation, get out of the house and work.

'You've forgotten the most important part,' she said, with irony. 'Don't you think I should also pray?' And she went off, before Joseph could answer. My master watched her for a long time as she went off because, now that the beautiful Dorothea had moved to Jerusalem, it was rare to see in Nazareth a more attractive way of walking. The body of Daniel's daughter exuded seduction.

Joseph now went out of his way to pass beneath the coppersmith's windows, whenever he left the house. He wasn't thinking of anything specific but he enjoyed the idea of the beautiful woman, ready to commit adultery with him. Daniel's Maria had noticed that he walked past her house, and she cast him big, dangerous smiles from behind the curtains. In the tradition of faithless husbands, Joseph brought his wife a present, a cornelian necklace.

Maria sensed the danger and began to follow him. She couldn't dismiss the thought of Daniel's Maria, as she had been that night in the shop, voluptuous, sinful; and our Maria blushed at the idea of Joseph in that woman's arms.

The day came when the seductress, instead of remaining at the window, waited at the street door. My master saw her and, at the same moment, saw his wife appear at the corner. He crossed the street, walking faster, as if he hadn't noticed either of the women.

This was enough: the awareness that Maria knew of his temptation and would have certainly found out if he were to break his vow of fidelity. He lost all inclination to go on with the game.

Neither he nor his wife said anything about the matter, wisely burying it in that storehouse of memory, where things should never be stirred up again.

At this time I discovered the fourth misfortune that had befallen Joseph, the worst yet.

One night I was sleeping against the wall of the house. Autumn was even more sultry than summer, and my shed was stifling. I woke because Joseph and his wife were leaning over the little parapet of the roof, talking, a few cubits above me. It seemed that she was rejecting her husband's embrace.

I heard Maria suggest an incredible thing to her husband: that he should go with another woman, in Ptolemais perhaps because she could absolutely not receive him in her bed. She spoke gently, sadly: it was clear that their marriage had not been consummated.

Joseph protested: he had promised to be faithful and he would be. Reasonably, she pointed out to him that when he had made that commitment neither he nor she had known that carnal union would be impossible, and that Joseph would be justified in seeking release with another woman. He refused again: 'I'm getting used to it,' he said, 'things are beautiful between us, even like this.'

She ran her hand through his hair, kissed his eyes, his forehead. 'You know, Joseph,' she said to him, 'that I love you more than anything in the world. You know that, don't you?'

I heard nothing more because they went back into the room. I was overwhelmed by that revelation. For a long time I sat there, indignant at fate, which was punishing my master so severely. No one better than I knew how much he liked women; and he, of all people, had to have a wife in name only, pregnant before the wedding, nobody knew by whom, and then for her to be inaccessible, sealed off . . .

I waited till they had fallen asleep, then climbed up to have a look. I peered cautiously into the bedroom: Maria was sleeping in the bed, Joseph on a mattress spread out on the floor; and presumably they had slept like this since the first night.

I didn't think of blaming Maria. I knew that this can happen: after her first and only sexual contact, surely forced on her with violence, she must have felt repugnance towards any man, even Joseph, whom she loved so much. And if he suffered, she must have been in despair at not being able to respond to her husband's desire.

Now I could understand their restraint at times, that forced, nervous aspect of their behaviour. I could understand Joseph's drinking, when he was racking his brain to figure out who had been responsible for his misfortune. And naturally I also interpreted his words, 'you still don't know the whole thing,' which had escaped him one drunken night. Forced chastity, plus a wife made pregnant by another man, was all he had got from his marriage.

I suffered for Joseph, but I also saw the comic side of his situation. I had envied him, trying not to betray my feelings, when all women were his; and now he didn't have a single one, not even his wife. If the girls of Bethlehem and Nazareth could see him in his present state, the handsome conqueror . . .

Poor Joseph. I realized he still had his illusions. In his opinion his wife's rejection of sexual contact was an effect of her pregnancy. After the delivery, the repugnance would fade, until it had completely disappeared. I could hear him repeat his conviction, like a magic formula: 'She'll get over it,' he would chant, handling the plane or the saw, convinced that no one could understand what he was talking about.

I admired Maria, who smiled even when she wanted to cry. Above all, it seemed a miracle to me that the two of them could maintain the love they felt for each other. Troubled but smiling, Maria was even more beautiful. Not ugly, but sad, my master no longer had the face of a victor, but was more like other men, including me.

After the unkind moment when I had laughed at his mishaps, I felt him even closer and more dear than in the past.

XI

Maria worked as before, but suddenly she would turn pale, her brow bathed in sweat. She agreed to rest only when Joseph forced her, and she would admit that she had to take care of herself for the baby's sake. She thought of him a great deal, speaking to him as if she wanted him to take part in the day's work.

'I've lined your cradle nicely,' she said to the unborn baby, 'but if it doesn't seem comfortable enough, tell me. Give me a little kick.' Or else she would say, 'I don't yet know what your favourite colour is. Green, perhaps. I'll paint the world green then: all the trees and meadows and edges of the roads will be green. Wherever you look, you'll see your colour.'

Joseph would shake his head and say: 'And what if he likes yellow? Or purple?'

It was a peaceful time. Perhaps because the husband in any case would have had to give up carnal relations with Maria, in her condition, and so his abstinence seemed to weigh less on him. And she, now close to her time, filled with the child about to be born, had thoughts for nothing else. Joseph followed her always with his eyes, took heavy objects from her hands, forced her to rest often on a special chair he had made for her. It seemed to him impossible that he had tormented her so much with his jealousy.

After she had been sitting for a moment, Maria stood up: she had seen something out of place, a lamp, a dish, and she hastened to put it right. Or else she didn't like the way a table-cloth had been folded: she went and folded it again. Joking, Joseph tied her to the chair by one ankle. The chair was very heavy. She forgot, and checked in her impulse, she would wave her arms the way a hen flaps her wings when she is held by the feet.

Maria sometimes thought about the physical reality of child-bearing, she remembered Elizabeth, her elderly relative, who had screamed for a whole night before the delivery; and she was afraid.

At the market she exchanged confidences with the older women, who had had children and knew what it meant. And especially with one of them, Michal, who had had a daughter only two months earlier.

'Does it really hurt that much?'

'Yes,' Michal said, with a self-important air, 'it's a terrible time.'

Maria wanted to know how long the pains had lasted, and if they were different before the birth and during it, and what they could be compared to. To the burning of a wound? To colic, to the nausea of indigestion? 'What are they like, I mean?'

Michal thought for a long time, then answered, honestly: 'I don't remember any more.' Maria was reassured.

Husband and wife, now at ease in their love for each other, occasionally teased, affectionately. He would imitate Maria's demure face months ago when she took part in the Sabbath stroll, and the way she signalled with her fingers; she would respond by imitating Joseph on horseback, proud of himself, and she would even repeat the movements of the horse, stomping and snorting, and the rider as he tried to control the animal, making sounds to calm him. In this double role, rapidly alternating to depict the equestrian group, Maria was irresistible. She would shake with her own laughter, finally, when she acted out dismounting, bending her knees slightly as she dropped to the ground, then depicting the restlessness of Saul (as she herself had named the horse), as he waited, tied to a ring in the wall.

This was the way they joked. But Maria was too young to know where to stop. Her gaiety, precisely because it was infrequent and precarious, led her to repeat the tricks she had played as a child, naturally at my expense and Nathan's.

She had discovered for example where the mute hid his wine-gourd. One day he raised the vessel over his face to send a spurt of his favourite beverage into his mouth, but a trickle of sand came from the gourd instead.

'It was you!' Nathan accused her, with signs, spitting sand

from his mouth. Disgusted, he went on coughing it up for a long time as we laughed.

One morning as I got out of bed, I stuck my feet into my sandals and tied the laces. After that, I stood up, took a first step, and fell to the ground on my face. Someone (and I knew who) with the complicity of someone else had nailed my sandals to the floor. At the thud of my fall, Maria and Joseph ran in, laughing. She brought me a new pair of sandals, which they gave me to replace the other ruined ones.

I always knew which of the pair had originally had the idea: the idea, for example, of the plank could have occurred only to him. He must have worked at it for a good part of the night, after having put a few drops of sleeping-draught in my wine, the way he used to in the past, when he didn't want me to discover his trysts with Dorothea.

One morning I took a plank from the pile in the courtyard; I needed it to fix a wagon. When I picked it up, another tilted slightly, making a third one also tilt, then a fourth, then all of them, until of that whole bunch of vertically stacked planks not one was still erect. It was a trick I had seen before, with bricks, or stiff tablets of parchment. But that wasn't all. As I looked in amazement at the little disaster I had caused, the last plank fell against a pile of logs, and that slight jar was enough to shift one of them, thus making the whole lot of them unstable. The logs started rolling down, accelerating because of the slope of the yard, sweeping away the poles supporting the laundry line. Maria, who had come to the door with Joseph, went on laughing in spite of the fact that all her washing was scattered over the yard, dirty once more.

'What of it? I'll wash it again,' she said, 'but I'll never see again the expression you had on your face when you thought you had caused all that earthquake!'

I couldn't even think of holding it against her and even less against Joseph. The joke played on him, those nights on the floor, was something far worse.

By now it was winter. Nathan dug a hibernating badger from his lair, and Maria cooked it in its own fat, filling the house with mouth-watering smells. The next day she and Joseph were to set off for Bethlehem.

Herod had issued an order that each of his subjects was to

return to his birthplace and be listed in the family rolls. When Cleophas was consulted, he came out in favour of civil disobedience, at least in theory. It was the Romans, he said, who wanted to take a census of the inhabitants of Palestine, and therefore in this case obeying the king meant recognizing the political authority of Rome. Counting the people is an operation expressly forbidden in Scripture; King David, when he wanted to know the number of his subjects, was punished by the Almighty for his vanity and pride. Herod had foreseen that the Romans' wish, if imposed directly on the populace, would cause riots; so he had replaced the emperor's decree with a law of his own.

Before his marriage, my master would surely have abstained; he would have disobeyed Herod's order and faced the consequences; but now, with the responsibility of Maria and the expected child, he gave up any idea of a fine gesture. He would go to Bethlehem and be enrolled.

Naturally, it wasn't necessary for Maria to go with him, she could have stayed at her uncle's house until her husband's return. But she was determined to go: the cold, the discomfort, the dangers didn't frighten her, as long as she could be with Joseph.

They held a kind of family council, with Cleophas and his wife present. Maria's uncle and aunt insisted she should stay at home with them. When he had run through the obvious arguments, the judge had recourse to unusual ones: 'Surely,' he said, 'you don't want your child to be born far from his home.'

'My child must be born in Judaea, in the land of his fathers.'

Maria spoke as if Joseph were the real father. Cleophas and his wife realized that she wanted to assume the fiction as truth, giving the child a guaranteed and respectable ancestry, graft him (if that's the expression) on to her husband's family tree. Joseph said nothing on this score; a shadow passed over his face, but I would have said he was content to take on that child, at least from the point of view of the registry. I realized, too, that this was exactly why she was insisting: so that Joseph would begin to feel, as far as possible, that the child was also his.

When they were alone, she sat on her husband's lap, as she had done when she was a girl; she didn't weigh much even now, with her swollen belly.

'If you don't want me to come, I won't,' she murmured.

'I'm worried for you. It's a hard journey. And here you would be safe, comfortable. Your aunt would be happy to take care of everything.'

She put her arm around his neck and whispered into his ear: 'I can't think of him being born when you aren't there. I would feel lost.' Joseph stroked her hair, which she had undone, allowing it to fall down her back. 'Please,' she went on, 'don't leave me. You know I've always relied on you, ever since I was little, ever since I was eight years old.'

In her voice there was the vibrant apprehension, the naked fear of a little girl. Joseph came to know a new sensation: that someone truly needed him. He promised to take her with him; after all, it was what he himself wanted. The idea of Maria's suffering birth-pains, without his being beside her to tend her, had already tormented him enough in the past few days, when he considered it his duty to go off and leave her behind. In spite of everything, he too couldn't live away from Maria.

They left together, and asked me to join them, with the duty of assisting them, while Nathan stayed behind to take care of the shop.

During the cold season it would have been unwise to take the low road, through the Jordan valley, because at times the river flooded; so we set off along the road that goes up and down over the mountain peaks, the same road that Joseph and I had taken coming here. Maria was riding an ass; we two men were on foot. There were many people on the move. In one way that was a reassurance (we joined a large group, which bandits and thieves wouldn't dare attack); on the other hand this multitude of travellers was worrisome. They were all going to our region, and it would be hard to find lodging in Bethlehem.

Nothing happened to us along the way; Maria seemed well, insofar as anyone can be well in that condition, except for one day when we had to stop, to give her time to recover from a fright. She was horrified on seeing a group of crucified men along the side of the road. It was the first time she had seen the cross, that instrument of torture and slow death, a barbarous invention of the Romans.

There were four crosses: three of the men were adults, the fourth was barely twenty. Two of them were already dead. Their skin was yellowish; where the executioners' clubs had shattered their bones it had become purple, or had been torn open in craters from which the rotting flesh erupted, full of worms. The raptor birds didn't descend on the corpses because the crosses were near the road, where people kept going past, and because the two live men frightened the birds off with their screams; but long grey rats climbed up along the wooden poles and clung to the bodies.

The twenty-year-old cried out in a hoarse voice, like someone who had been protesting for hours against the death to which he had been condemned. They hadn't clubbed his legs, but he was half-crazed: the cold wind and the sun had seared him. His eyes were two red holes, weeping blood; his lips were cracked. The boy shook his head from left to right and from right to left, never stopping; the rest of his body was motionless, rigid. Life had become for him one endless cry, and a movement of negation.

The last man, about forty, must have been crucified only a short time before: he still had enough breath left to rail at people. He asserted his innocence, he said he was neither a brigand nor a thief, but a prophet; and this could easily have been the truth.

Maria felt ill. I had never seen a face as pale as hers was then. She held out for a little while, as we hastened to get away from that spectacle, then she began to scream and wave her arms and legs convulsively. We managed to calm her only by stopping and stretching her out beside a fire.

I remember Joseph, looking at her, aghast, and she said to him: 'If I see another cross, I will die of it.'

That night, lying in the straw in a stable, dressed, covered with cloaks, neither Joseph nor his wife could sleep. Maria was still trembling; in the end she clasped her husband and clung to him in desperation, telling him that she loved him. She didn't relax her arms' grip until she fell asleep, but she would wake from time to time and seize him again.

We arrived after three days' walking; it was almost night, and the air was very cold. We found no room in the inn or anywhere else. What was worse, the labour pains had begun.

The child was born in a stable where we had taken shelter. (Joseph knew that the little building, isolated in the midst of the countryside, belonged to his brothers, but, as he said, this was a case of necessity.) Luckily, the baby was born quickly and well: a boy, red and angry. Still, those were painful moments. I had never seen a woman give birth, and neither had Joseph. With anguish, we watched Maria suffering, crying out like an animal, unable to restrain herself. The worst feeling was our own helplessness.

Joseph held her hands, and in her torment she dug her nails into his flesh. He sent me off to find a midwife. When I came back without having found one, late at night, I was hoping that Maria had already given birth: and, in fact, the child was born. I heard his crying from the distance, and I ran the last part of the way.

Some shepherds, who were keeping a flock not far off, seeing the fire we had lighted outside the stable to heat water, had come to take a look. They returned a little later, bringing us milk, cheese, and bread. With them were two women, who stayed to help Maria.

I went outside. The moon was shining down on the fields; my footsteps echoed, the way they do when the ground is frozen. I heard the child's voice; he wasn't crying, but was rather shouting, proclaiming to the world that now he was also here, the way all infants do.

It was impossible to stay outside very long: it was too cold.

Maria was fine, but we couldn't set off for the homeward journey, because according to the law she was impure: she had to stay in retirement for forty days, then offer a sacrifice to the Lord, after which she would be free to go wherever she pleased. The child was circumcized: an expert in these operations came, made the incision, tore the membrane, sucked the blood, and sprinkled on the wound a mixture of oil, wine, and cumin. The little one yelled as if they were disembowelling him.

In this country they set great store by being circumcized, because Greeks and Romans aren't; and so what might be only a hygienic practice has become a badge, a statement of nationality. Joseph bought two doves to offer in sacrifice, he was to pay also five silver shekels to the temple, to ransom the infant, when they went for the presentation, for the first-born of men and of animals belong to the Lord.

Foreseeing that their stay in Bethlehem would be extended, Joseph went to Manasseh and asked his permission to remain in the stable. Years had passed since their separation, and Manasseh no longer bore his old grudge against his brother. He gladly gave Joseph permission and offered him money, as a loan or a gift, if he needed any. My master refused.

Meanwhile, I made a little tour of the local stables, hoping to see someone of my acquaintance. I found only a certain Eli, a drinking companion in the old days. He was now working in Jerusalem, in the palace of Herod, but he came back here when he could, to see his parents. I knew that he owed my master some money.

'When are you going to pay?' I asked him.

'One of these days,' he said, replying with the words of all insolvent creditors. 'One of these days I'll pay it back, with interest.'

Joseph called me, to come back, just when I had found one of the kitchen maids who in the old days had had a weakness for me.

In the knowledge that physical union was impossible (for forty days a new mother is untouchable), Maria and Joseph allowed their tenderness free rein. She would lie for a long time on the blankets and cloaks, and Joseph would bring her a flower he had found in the snow, a harbinger of spring, or a little, half-frozen bird that had to be nourished and kept warm until it could fly again. She swore that the infant, only a few days old, could see the creature.

Joseph also shared her enthusiasm for the baby, partly because my master had a father's heart, but mostly because it was the only way he could feel at one with her.

Maria was always with the baby, changing it, nursing it. During the rare moments when the baby was asleep (I had the sensation that he never slept at all), she knelt down beside him and stayed there looking at him, as he lay in a manger that made a fine crib.

'And when I think,' Maria said to her husband, 'how you had prepared such a beautiful cradle for him, with no nails, all inlaid and polished . . .'

Who knows? Perhaps if he had had a bed that rocked the baby might have slept more. He would seem peaceful, sunk in deep sleep, and then he would suddenly wake up screaming. He couldn't have been hungry, because he had just had his feed. Maria took him in her arms, sang him a lullaby. Finally he would quiet down; we would all move cautiously in total silence. His mother would put him down and at that same moment the baby would yell his lungs out again. And Maria would pick him up and rock him some more.

She was exhausted. Joseph, too. I went to sleep with our shepherd friends, when I couldn't stand the little nuisance any longer; but my master stayed there with his wife. It served no purpose, that sacrifice of his, except to show his solidarity: perhaps it was also a help to her, knowing he was near. She was worn out, her forehead was damp with sweat, but her tenderness in caring for her son never faltered. To tell you the truth, or what seemed to me the truth, Maria didn't love the baby, she worshipped him, she would adore him on her knees as if he were a little god. It was immediately apparent that she was experiencing motherhood for the first time.

Finally, washed, changed, fed his fill, her son fell asleep. Maria lay down on the straw. Joseph caressed her; she turned and hid her face against his shoulder.

To rule that two people in love must not love each other carnally is a real injustice. Maria's illness was rare and hard to understand. I had a relative in the same situation. Her husband, whom she loved, wouldn't give up. The moment he touched her, the woman would cry out and have convulsions. And he persisted in his attempts so much that the poor woman went crazy.

At that time, Joseph and Maria, who couldn't have lain together in any case, were like everyone else, like other young couples who had just had a child. I would leave the stable so they could kiss and hug at their ease.

When I told Joseph about my meeting with Eli, he just shrugged: he had long since given up all hope of getting his money back. But Eli then sought Joseph out, not to repay the loan but to give him some advice that was much more valuable.

In Herod's palace he had got wind of a horrible expedition, a slaughter that was to occur. Soldiers were going to surround the Bethlehem territory and kill all children under the age of two. Then Herod would go off for the baths at Callirrhoe. By bringing Joseph this news my friend knew he was risking his own life.

Maria wouldn't believe it. 'Why should the king have anything against babies?'

'Remember,' Joseph said, 'that Herod had his own son killed. He's old and sick. It wouldn't be the first time a king tried to put a river of blood between himself and death.'

The next morning he announced, opportunely, that he had dreamed of an angel. The Almighty's messenger bade them to leave. And so Maria was also convinced.

In any case, there was nothing to keep them: the period of impurity was over, the child had been presented in the temple.

Maria asked only: 'Where will we go?'

'The farther, the better. We'll go to Egypt.'

I remembered that Joseph had long wanted to cross the desert and know the country from which his forefathers had fled many years before.

There were no solemn farewells. I was sent back to look after the house and shop. 'We'll see you in a couple of months,' Joseph said.

Everyone knows what happened then in Bethlehem: the famous massacre of the innocents will be recorded in the history books. Maria's son was one of the few who escaped.

XII

Joseph had spoken of a two months' absence; he stayed in Egypt for eight years, until Herod died and all danger had vanished. I had news from him a couple of times; I heard he had stopped at Leontopolis, a city full of his compatriots. He probably didn't feel like an exile because in Egypt there are many, many sons of Israel; for that matter they are dispersed all over the place, in Phoenicia, in Syria, in Asia Minor, in Thessaly, Macedonia, Aetolia, Attica, in the Peloponnesus, and there are large settlements in Alexandria and in Rome.

My master knew a trade and he found a way to earn his living, without having to give up the habits he had acquired at home, maintaining his sabbath rest and attending meetings at the synagogue. Left in Nazareth to keep things going, I, on the contrary, encountered many difficulties. Nathan went back to being a shepherd. Now that Joseph was gone, Nathan saw no reason to work for somebody else. Nobody would give me credit any more: I am uncircumcized. And then I had to pay a fine to the parents of a girl who was quicker than I was . . . But I want to tell Joseph's story here, not my own.

My master came home on a summer day, towards evening. I was sitting outside the door of the shop, taking the cool air, and I saw him come in from the street (the gate always stood open): him, Joseph, pushing forward a little grey ass loaded with bundles; then Maria, then the boy, holding his mother's hand. They were all dusty, dead tired.

Joseph embraced me, and so did Maria. Eight years hadn't changed my master a great deal: he was just calmer, less impatient than in his youth. Maria had become even more beautiful: mature, serene.

I brought water to wash their feet. The boy took the basin from my hand and washed his mother's feet himself. He was tall for his age; he looked neither like Maria nor like Joseph, with his light hair and blue eyes.

Helping them carry up their bundles and unpack them, I realized that Joseph hadn't made his fortune: their linen, their tunics, the sheets were old and patched. And yet he must have worked hard: his hands were covered with a uniform layer of calluses.

Work began to come in again as the word that Joseph was back gradually spread. But those were lean years. The harvest was scant, and most of our customers were farmers. There wasn't much money around, and the little family led a humble life, like poor people. Maria and Joseph were still young, and undaunted. He would whistle as he worked, and she would sing, as she kept busy in the next room. The child, who was named Jesus, went to the synagogue school and, in his free hours, after he had run around the yard a bit, he came into the shop to lend a hand. He was rather good at the job: his father had taught him in Egypt. The child had an extraordinary instinctive feeling for wood: he could look at a log and tell you right off if it was the kind to be sawed into planks, if the knots were deep or only on the surface; he described the veins inside as if he could see them before his eyes. He seemed destined for the craft, by a vocation, as it had been with Joseph. But (and this was his mother's opinion and desire) it was also possible that he would become a scribe or a doctor of the Law. The teacher at the synagogue said he learned rapidly: he already knew a good part of the Holy Books.

The only trouble was that he was never satisfied with the traditional interpretation, the fruit of the knowledge of distinguished masters; he insisted on explaining even the most difficult passages in his own way. He argued, boldly defending his point of view. These displays of arrogance and presumption upset and shocked his teacher.

Jesus was one of those people you love out of admiration, not out of affinity. When he smiled, he radiated charm just as Joseph had, in his day. The boy certainly didn't resemble my master, blond as he was and with light eyes: I realized that he resembled instead the man Joseph had imagined when he hid in the wood shed to catch Maria's presumed seducer and saw him in his mind's eye coming through the gate into the yard.

That imaginary man also was blond and had blue eyes.

The coincidence must have struck Joseph, too, for every now and then in the shop he would pause for a moment, look at the boy, then shake his head. I realized that Maria had maintained her silence and hadn't revealed to him who the other man was.

Jesus slept by himself in a little room created for him by putting a wooden partition in the big ground-floor room next to the shop, and the husband and wife went upstairs to sleep. I observed that Joseph still lay on a mattress placed at the foot of the bed: Maria had not been cured. I knew what torture that enforced chastity must have been for my master during the eight years of exile. By then renunciation had become a habit. You can adjust to anything, even to the loss of an arm or a leg. Every now and then, all the same, his abstinence was a burden to him again. Sexual desire caused an exasperation in Joseph that transformed him. Dishevelled, fierce, he would roam through the house and yard like a cat in heat; he would sleep outdoors, plunge his face into the bucket of water. It would pass in a couple of days, and Joseph would be the man he usually was, calm and smiling, but weak, as if he had experienced in reality the lascivious scenes that unfolded in his imagination.

Even more attractive with his flowing beard, an adult with experience of life, elegant when he took some pains with his appearance, he caught the eyes of the wives and widows of Nazareth. The girls, on the other hand, looked past him, without lingering: at thirty, Joseph was an old man for them, and married, too. But he succumbed to the girls' fascination, as in the old days; he followed them in the street, when they went to the synagogue with their mothers, he admired the trim ankles, the curve of the hips below the belt. He observed them as if they were a show: Joseph loved his wife.

I had not been surprised to find that things between the two had remained as they were; I knew that Maria's illness was incurable; but I was sincerely amazed that my master had managed to remain chaste. He said to me one day that, in this respect, he felt like a man in prison, under a life sentence.

We were sitting on the steps of the synagogue, in the shade, watching the people going inside. A beautiful woman went by, Maria daughter of Daniel, who had tried to trick Joseph into marrying her and had failed. It was known around the town that, though she was married, she wouldn't say no to anyone who appealed to her; and Joseph, it was clear, still appealed to her, at least to judge by the way she looked at him. Under that stare, Joseph lowered his eyes, embarrassed.

There was a dialogue between them, only half-spoken, that nobody else would have been able to understand.

As I also followed the woman's lithe form, as she entered that place of prayer and meeting, I winked at Joseph and said: 'Why not?'

'No,' he replied, firmly.

I repeated: 'Why not?'

'I swore a vow,' he said.

'I know, but . . . ' I wanted to say to him that when he had solemnly sworn to be faithful to Maria, he had no idea he was marrying a woman who would keep him from her bed; and therefore he could consider himself released from his oath. Joseph knew that I knew.

He murmured, almost to himself: 'That's what she says, too, but then . . . ' By now I could understand his slightest hint, and I guessed what he was thinking: he was afraid that, if he did give way, Maria would lose much of her respect for him. The only way in which he could still seem an exceptional man in his wife's eyes was by resisting temptation. At this point sexual abstinence had become not only a habit but almost an obsession, a choice, which at times gave him serenity, an air of wisdom. He may not have been happy, but managing to hold out was also a satisfaction, and he was proud of it.

I knew what it cost him, especially on the days when his desire was reawakened, and I realized, too, how great Maria's power over him was, if for her sake he was able to remain chaste. But why did he expose himself to temptation by looking at the girls?

'They are beautiful,' he said, 'but I still haven't seen one more beautiful than Maria.' His sacrifice was great, but he was offering it to an exceptional woman; and this, for him, was another source of pride.

After eight years their life together had, every now and then, some dark areas. At times, a word, a trifle was enough to bring on Joseph's quarrelsome mood. Maria didn't answer back, but often her air of forced meekness irritated Joseph more than an angry reply would have.

Most times the cause of their disagreement was Jesus. In my opinion the boy had only one serious failing: other boys his age were silent unless they had been questioned. He talked. Not that he was a chatterbox, but he always wanted to express his views. Joseph had made the mistake of not teaching the child his place at the outset, and now he joined in the grownups' talk.

When we weren't able to catch him and put him to work, Jesus behaved like a little vagabond: he wandered around the city, preferably alone or with a bunch of little idlers his own age. He explored the hills near Nazareth, visited the gardens looking for fruit, often driven off and chased by the owners. He came home covered with dust and sweat, tattered, breathless. Maria filled a tub in the yard with water and washed him from head to foot. She rubbed soap over him and cleansed him gently; with him her gestures were always tender and loving.

The relationship between the boy and my master changed in the first year of their return. At the beginning Jesus was very attached to Joseph, paying attention to everything his father said or did, looking at him with admiration, telling him how handsome he was. My master was very proud of him, not saitisfied with having him always in sight in the shop, he took the boy with him whenever he went out: into the countryside to deliver ploughs and yokes, or to the mountains to buy wood. Jesus drank in his father's words.

At a certain point, however, he began expressing his own viewpoint, contradicting Joseph, and often without giving sufficient reason.

'And who says that's how it is?' his father challenged him.

'I say so.'

Joseph, hearing the child quite seriously employ that tone of authority that he himself had often used with the child, burst out laughing.

Jesus continued to be dutiful towards him, but only on the surface; once free with words and questions, now the boy became tight-tipped.

Joseph suffered at that. Precisely because he wasn't the boy's real father, he wanted all the more for Jesus to consider himself Joseph's son. Joseph didn't want just obedience from him, but also trust, love. It seemed, on the contrary, that the child had abolished within himself any idea of having a father on this earth, to consider himself only a son of God.

One day in the shop Joseph put his arm on the boy's shoulder, as he was in the habit of doing, affectionately, and was hurt when Jesus said to him: 'Please, don't touch me.' His voice was the same as ever, not annoyed or hostile, perfectly inexpressive. Taking his arm from the boy's shoulder, my master felt that his protection was being refused, that he was becoming a useless father.

Then he made a mistake: he tried to win the boy back. For a fairly long period, as his son was growing and feeling more and more self-sufficient, Joseph began to display towards him all his old resources of charm. He paid attention again to his appearance; but most of all, he tried to be a companion to his son, not an older man, a brother rather than a father.

Maria observed all this with an impassive smile. Jesus, seeing how Joseph was trying to ingratiate himself, turned more than ever to his mother.

The boy and Maria understood each other without words; there was never the slightest conflict between them: they seemed to enter, one into the other, to form a single person, their understanding was so close.

I had noticed, for example, a strange thing: whenever the child came into the house, he never asked, 'Where's Mama?' He always knew where to find her and would go straight to that place, without hesitation: to the chicken coop, at the end of the yard, to the upper room, to the garden. If anything happened to Jesus, she would sense it, even at a distance. One day I saw her turn pale and lean against a wall; she pressed her hands to her side and moaned. Her son came home towards evening, with his hand at the same place: he had quarrelled with his comrades and had received a severe blow. The time that Maria slipped on the outside steps and rolled all the way down, striking her head on the stones, they had barely laid her on the kitchen table when he appeared, distressed, panting. We were very worried, because Maria seemed close to death: she was very pale and her pulse was throbbing weakly.

'Get up, Mama,' Jesus said; he couldn't bear the sight of sick people. And Maria sat up. 'Walk.' And she slipped down from the table and began to walk in the room.

Joseph ran to support her; he didn't want Maria to fall again, just to satisfy her son. In fact, he scolded Jesus: 'Can't you see we should let her lie down, calmly? Standing up like this, she could have an attack, when the blood goes to her head.' He also scolded Maria: 'What are you doing? All he has to do is open his mouth and you're all well again. No, you must take care. Go to bed now.'

Maria said there was no need and, to prove it, she began to run around the table, chasing Jesus, who darted off. They were both laughing, uttering little cries of excitement. Joseph, feeling excluded, left the house, slamming the door.

Joseph got his own back by teaching the boy masculine games and behaviour. He taught him how to defend himself in a fight, how to jump walls by pressing down your hands and swinging your legs sideways, how to whistle, how to swim. He even took him to the tavern. That time Maria got angry: it's probably the only time I saw her really irritated.

When the boy had already gone off to sleep, she accused Joseph of wanting to ruin him. She allowed herself to reveal that she understood things far more than was apparent: 'You're doing this because you want to separate him from me.'

'As far as I'm concerned,' he replied, 'you can keep him. Of course, he's only yours.'

Maria bowed her head and burst into tears.

Joseph used to slip a few coins to Jesus from time to time, so the boy could go and buy cakes from Abel the baker. Proud as he was, the boy didn't welcome these gifts and would usually refuse them; but he liked sweets, so on occasion he would accept the money and run to Abel's. He would spend every last penny on cakes, and Joseph would take the opportunity to reproach him for not having set anything aside and to preach the virtue of saving.

'You'll never have anything of your own, if you don't learn to accumulate money.'

'What for?' the boy replied, unconvinced. 'I have everything I need. What would I buy with the money I saved?'

'I don't know . . . a tunic . . . '

'I already have one.'

' . . . a cloak . . . '

'I have that old one of yours. Mama is shortening it for me.'

He never told his mother about these little orgies of cakes; but he didn't eat them in secret and he never failed to offer her some. Simply neither he nor she found anything to say about the fact that a good father bought sweets for his son.

Maria was offended because once Joseph made the mistake of saying to Jesus, as he put the money in the boy's pocket: 'Not a word to your mother, mind you.'

She sulked, but as she was usually quiet at table, it took Joseph a while to realize she wasn't speaking to him. 'What's wrong?' he asked her. 'What's happened?', far from imagining the reasons for that ill-humour of hers. She didn't answer: she smiled in that mysterious way of hers, which had the effect of a rainbow on Joseph, and said nothing of the reasons for her mood. Now the skies were clear again. In an equally mysterious way, my master sensed her mute reproach, and after that he never asked his son to conceal anything from his mother.

One evening the boy kept teasing his mother, begging her to tell about her own childhood, the games she used to play, and with whom. Maria answered, briefly, and a bit shyly, but she was amused and vaguely moved by those memories. She revealed that the most beautiful plaything she had ever had was a little cart, which Joseph had built for her in the yard of an inn, at Bethlehem.

'Do you still have it?'

Unfortunately, from hard use, the wheels had worn out, the axles had bent, the little cart no longer existed. Maria described the thrill of letting it carry her down a slope, as she held on to the strings that directed the little vehicle, like a horse's reins.

Joseph worked late that night, and when Jesus woke up he found a new little cart, with wheels of hard wood, at the foot of his bed. He thanked Joseph with enthusiasm, flinging his arms around his neck; then he disappeared, pulling his present after him. Nazareth has many sloping streets; Jesus had only to choose. Probably he tried them all out, because he came back home with a bump on his head, the result of a difficult curve. He was late for supper, covered with dust from head to foot, but beaming.

He wouldn't give Joseph a moment's peace until he taught him how to build little carts. Then, with his father's help, he built another three for friends of his. The four boys would race one another down the streets, passing and colliding, as they shouted with joy. The little carts became a popular game, the desire of every child. Fathers came to Joseph to order the newly-invented vehicle (which was actually not new at all) for their sons; my master built little carts and charged for them. But it took him so much time that he didn't earn much money from them.

It would have taken far more than that to recoup the fortunes of the shop. Our work brought in barely enough to keep us alive and any unusual expenditure was decided after suitable deliberation. For example, little Jesus needed a new tunic: the old one was not only faded and patched, but the seams no longer held. Maria said at table that she would cut down one of his father's old ones.

'No, no, poor Jesus,' my master said. 'Those are all patches, too. Must he always go around looking like a beggar? He must have a new tunic.'

'There's no money, you know that. And perhaps he doesn't care.'

Indeed, Jesus said: 'What does it matter? I don't even notice what I'm wearing.'

Still he was given the new tunic. To tell the truth, he wasn't very grateful for the present. The brand-new garment intimidated him because his mother had told him to take care not to tear it or soil it. He did tear it, finally, in a fall from the cart. Jesus was scolded, but he felt some relief. Once it had been patched, the tunic was no longer new, and he could play freely, even when he was wearing it.

XIII

'The Lord be with you,' Jesus said, greeting us, as he sat down, the last to come to the table. He was late again.

'And what about you? Are you sure the Lord is with you? If he were your father, in my place, he'd give you a good walloping.'

'You can do that yourself,' Jesus said, ready to accept any punishment Joseph inflicted on him.

'Is that any way to answer me? Who do you think you are?' Now that he had started, my master went on complaining. 'A young gentleman, the head of the house, the master of the world, to come and go as you please? I'll tell you what you are: a swellhead, who thinks he's better than his mother and me; an ingrate, who doesn't care a fig about the sacrifices we make. You're an idler, a rogue, a vagabond. You'll come to a bad end, I tell you.'

Jesus hung his head, looking at his plate, without answering.

'To say nothing . . . ' his father went on, ' . . . of all the times that instead of going to school you go out into the fields. I can't tell you how many people have complained to me about you and that band of jackasses you run around with. You fight, you damage the gardens, you steal fruit . . . '

'Only windfalls,' Jesus said, interrupting.

The interruption arrested that flow of accusations. Joseph looked at the boy, ten years old by now, and felt deeply insulted by the child's calm. Jesus didn't get angry, but replied like an equal; he didn't cry when he was scolded; rather, with his little smile of docile submission, he succeeded in letting his father know that the accusations were all true and all irrelevant; he was listening to the words, but he let them pass over him, light as a breeze.

Sometimes Joseph beat him; that is to say, he gave the boy a couple of slaps, the minimum number for a paternal punishment; but he went no farther. He was afraid that his authority, affirmed with hesitation and accepted without any conviction, might be challenged. He even avoided sending Jesus from the table when the boy's insolent serenity exasperated him.

A year before, he had done it. 'Leave the table,' he had said. He expected the child would follow the customs observed in the families of Israel since time immemorial, that he would retire to his little room or behind the sheds, to weep and recover from his shame. But Jesus, interpreting the order in a broader sense, more suitable to his purposes, had left the house. He didn't return for two days, after living off unripe fruit, grasses, and locusts. He enjoyed himself hugely. On the third day he reappeared in the yard, chiefly out of love for his mother. She was the one who insisted he ask Joseph's pardon which the boy did gladly.

'Have you repented?' Joseph asked. 'Your mother was dying of grief.'

'I'm truly sorry for that.'

'But you don't repent running away?'

'How can I repent having obeyed you? You told me to leave, and I left.' And so Jesus received another couple of slaps for having been disrespectful to his father.

Frequently, if there was a wounded or abandoned creature around Jesus would take it in. In one corner of the yard he kept a dog with a broken leg, a blind kitten, a dove that couldn't fly, and even a little vixen, hurt by a trap. His playmates were all the dirtiest, ugliest outcasts of the city; he spent his time with vagabonds and beggars, old women who had no one left in the world.

My master, as was only natural, didn't approve Jesus's tendency to make friends with the refuse of society.

'You'll never get ahead in life that way,' he said to the boy. 'Who will you ask for help when you need a recommendation? Why don't you make friends with respectable boys? The son of the tax-collector, who is your age; or the son of judge Habinadab?'

Obediently Jesus promised he would spend time also with that other part of Nazarene society, and he kept his word: he had an extraordinary gift for making friends with anyone. The boys from the city's good families joined his little band, discovering the joy of getting dirty, then going home, timid, fearing punishment, but secretly proud of their skinned knees or broken noses. Where could they have found anyone more fun to play with, a friend who allowed even the newcomers to be David or Samson in the fights (half wars and half play-acting) organized by Jesus's band every day up on the hills?

Jesus invented the rules of the games, which tended to restrain the spirit of competition; otherwise the boys, in their enthusiasm, would really have hurt themselves.

The desire to compete with his son had begun tormenting Joseph again. When his attempt to win the boy back had failed, and he saw it was hopeless to try to hold him at that age when he still needed paternal protection, my master now took the field, prepared to compete, to become an object of admiration and envy in Jesus's eyes. He could still, naturally, defeat him in their tame wrestling, kicks and blows barred, in the courtyard at dusk, while they were waiting to be called to supper; but in other contests the outcome remained doubtful or tended to be in the boy's favour.

In the evening they would play at ninepins with the balls that Joseph had patiently made from an old oak log. Though they were carefully rounded, the balls followed an irregular path, bouncing over the uneven terrain. Joseph, out of patience, tried hard shots and often missed his aim. Jesus's bowls, on the contrary, struck home every time. As soon as he picked up the wooden ball, it seemed bewitched. While Joseph would make some ironic comment on Jesus's shot, the ball would come to a pebble, correct its course, bounce on a hole farther on, turn left or right, and unfailingly reach the pins, always knocking over more than one.

I couldn't help laughing when I saw Joseph take aim so carefully and throw the balls with such power, always achieving unfortunate results; whereas Jesus seemed to throw at random always hitting the target.

Joseph was a bad loser, and he would insist on another game, to have his turn to win. Maria volunteered to play with her husband before it was dark and she would lose in order to restore his self-confidence. Sometimes the trick worked and Joseph would regain all his old verve; at other times his defeat left him bitter and dejected, a prey to self-pity, quarrelsome.

He would sit down to supper with his wife and son, and it seemed to him that both were pitying him, also failing in the respect due him as head of the household.

It's true that Maria chiefly looked after Jesus. It was her fault that the boy had become the most important person in the family. He liked to eat well, for example, and his mother paid heed first to his tastes, doing everything possible to prepare from the scant resources of our larder the dishes he liked best.

Sometimes she even forgot precedence and served him first. Joseph would react with acid irony. 'When you have a moment,' he said, 'I hope you'll put something on my plate, too. Perhaps you didn't notice that I'm also here.'

Maria would blush and apologize. Jesus passed his plate to his father. Then Joseph, ashamed, would eat nothing, vaguely displeased with himself, too. The boy said to him: 'Eat something, or else Mama will cry,' and Joseph would eat.

My master acted the victim, especially when he had lost at ninepins. He would accuse his wife of neglecting him, on the slightest pretext, saying she no longer showed him the same consideration as she had in the early days.

The soup was cold (and it was the fault of Joseph, who had lingered in the courtyard), there was a stain on the tablecloth, they hadn't set his usual chair at his place; any trifle sufficed to unleash my master's complaints and charges.

'You hardly notice whether or not I'm present,' he would begin. 'Who do you think I am? A substitute father? The poor relation?'

He lacked the heart to go on: she looked at him with such pleading affection, with such total devotion that he lost entirely that desire to wound her, which had come over him before.

Maria answered him back only when it was a matter of something serious, like the future of Jesus.

Joseph was tired of being told by other people that his son was a rascal and an idler. 'I'll set him to work all day in the shop,' he threatened. 'That way he'll learn the craft properly.'

He hadn't the slightest doubt that Jesus would be a carpenter, and a good one. In those few hours that he succeeded in keeping the boy from his roaming, Jesus worked like a grown man, even with pleasure, because everything came out well for him, and he seemed to enjoy himself.

'That isn't his trade,' his mother said.

Joseph insisted. First of all, the job of carpenter seemed right for Jesus, who was talented and would come into a shop in good working order; and besides, Joseph could see no reason for ignoring the custom of handing down a profession from father to son.

'After all,' he said, out of patience, 'in your opinion, what should we make of this boy? He's ten years old and already a scandal in the neighbourhood: he doesn't go to school, roams the countryside, is involved in at least one fight a day . . . You tell me: what are we to do with him? What do you suggest?'

'People don't understand him,' Maria said. 'What he does is always prompted by good intentions. What do they accuse him of, specifically? They say he's a rascal, but has anyone ever come and charged him with a misdeed, a theft, an act of bullying? They say he's a vagabond, but is it a crime to be young and feel like running free? And as for the fighting, you know as well as I do that Jesus never fights except to defend the weak . . . '

'Defending the weak isn't a trade,' Joseph grumbled, 'or, if it is, it surely doesn't bring in enough to eat on. If you take the side of the beggars, the people who matter will be against you, and often the very people you protect will turn against you, too; they're never satisfied. Not even if you work miracles will you become somebody . . . As long as it's a matter of playing ninepins, Jesus is a champion, I admit; but in everything else, he's a boy like any other.'

'Are you really sure he's like any other boy?' Maria hinted.

'If you really want to know, I'll tell you: often he's worse than the others, and often he's better. With him, there's never any telling what sort of man he'll become. He'll be a vagabond also when he's grown up.'

'Why don't we ask him the question, what he'll be when he's a man?'

Asked, Jesus said that when the time came he would know what to do. Meanwhile, he implied, they should let him live in his own way, which included running over the hills, being involved in fights, slipping away from the house. He disappeared periodically for a couple of days, and there was never any knowing where he went or what he did; his companions didn't know, either. Now that he could write, he would leave a few words for Maria, scrawled on a pottery shard with a piece of coal. But she worried all the same. When he came home and she asked him questions, he didn't answer, or else answered rudely.

'I have my own business to attend to,' he said to her once, meaning that the others should also mind their own business, without invading the little area of privacy he had created for himself.

Nathan the mute (who now owned a large flock and was kept very busy) came to visit us only rarely, but Judge Cleophas often appeared in the yard. Maria's uncle was going through a period of decline. His wife had died, and she had been the real support of the family; he had been left not so much a widower as an orphan. With only an old maidservant in the big house, he spent his time dozing, not bothering to wash or to get dressed. He had become querulous and would start an argument at the tavern with anyone who had the patience to heed him.

'If only your great-aunt were alive,' he said to Jesus, 'she would make you a cake: she was wonderful in the kitchen and she also knew all sorts of fairy-tales.'

Cleophas had lost many things but not his curiosity. In secret, he followed Jesus during his escapades, then reported all at home. Jesus sometimes realized he was being followed, but paid no attention, not to spoil the old man's pleasure in spying.

'I don't understand this great-nephew of mine,' Cleophas said to the boy's parents, with his accustomed solemnity; and he told how he had seen Jesus fight with some other boys, not members of his band, but bigger youths. It seemed they were fighting over a nest of birds that the older boys had pulled down from a tree. Now, set on the grass, it would presumably go to the winner.

'It wasn't a brawl: it was single combat, one against one,' the judge continued. One after another, Jesus had forced two of his opponents to surrender. Those left had abandoned the field.

'And then he did something that, if I hadn't seen, I wouldn't have believed. He went back up the hill, climbed a tree, and set the nest in the cleft of two branches, the place it had been taken from.'

Cleophas had approached, acting like a man out for a stroll

on his own, and had waited for the boy at the foot of the tree. 'What are you doing?' he had asked him then.

'I was giving the nest back to the birds who made it.'

Cleophas's legal mind could only agree that Jesus's motivation was good and just, even if it went against usual behaviour and against the instinct of country boys: there could be no doubt about the true ownership of the nest, but it had never before occurred to him that the question should be considered from the birds' point of view.

Jesus came home late, taking care not to be seen by his father. Maria washed his bruises, his little wounds, so that he could appear at the supper table without causing too much alarm. Noticing that Jesus was in worse shape than on other evenings, Joseph started one of his scenes.

He began with an apparently innocuous question: 'Have you seen the state in which your son turns up at table?'

In these situations, fathers say 'your son' as if momentarily rejecting paternity and tacitly accusing their wives of not having properly brought up the guilty party, almost of being his accomplice in his bad behaviour. Joseph, too, had no other intention, but in his position those words could take on another meaning. He realized this when Maria stood up, her eyes filled with tears, and left the table. This had never happened before, and for this reason Joseph realized that he had truly wounded her.

He went to her, to ask her forgiveness. By now Maria's premarital mischance had become the secret torment of them both, and it united them more than it divided them. They had no need for words, especially since Maria knew perfectly well that her husband's expression had been involuntary. They embraced at once, warmly. She wept, consoled, on Joseph's shoulder, and he stroked her hair.

Little Jesus had the qualities of a leader. The boys who followed him tacitly acknowledged his leadership; the poor and the outcasts who had placed themselves in his hands obeyed him as a chief. And yet he didn't act like someone who imposes himself on others: he didn't give orders, never raised his voice: he confined himself to expressing an opinion or a wish and his friends behaved accordingly.

There was a time when the adults he had helped became a

little band, six people who previously had roamed about the city and the nearby villages, each on his own; they collected around him not out of necessity, but from choice. They were not pretty to look at: there was Jeremiah the hunchback, Achimelech, who had a prominent goitre; a cripple, Abraham; Jonathan the idiot; and two women, the witch Noemi and old Esther who, in her heyday, had been a famous prostitute. Noemi was old, too; she could give a sheep worms and could wave her hand and put a woman to sleep, if she found one alone in a farmhouse, which she could then rob in her own good time.

Jesus had come upon Jeremiah one day in a deserted alley below the walls; the hunchback had threatened him with a knife in order to steal the piece of bread Jesus was eating.

'Put away your knife and I'll give it to you,' the boy had said, 'and I'll give you a drachma as well.'

The other man raised his weapon, more to frighten the child than to threaten him, but Jesus didn't move. On the contrary, he smiled and said: 'Surely you don't want to stab me for a piece of bread.'

'Give it to me.'

'Put away your knife and I'll give it to you.'

In this kind of verbal duel Jesus always won. I had figured out why, too: he smiled, as if he were enjoying himself, and his adversary, disconcerted, would give in.

The boy and the hunchback became friends. Jesus had a try at bringing Jeremiah to sleep in our yard, but Joseph wouldn't have it: dogs, doves, foxes, yes; humans, no. It was hard for the child to see the logic about taking animals in need of care and affection into the house, while human beings were rejected. Still, as an obedient son, he accepted his father's decree and sought another lodging for Jeremiah.

Actually, the hunchback insisted he didn't need any: like the other homeless, he slept in barns and, during the summer, in ditches. Jesus insisted, and with a bundle of straw made Jeremiah a bed in an abandoned house, crumbling and full of nettles, where people threw their refuse. The new dwelling needed thorough cleaning so the boys in Jesus's group devoted themselves to the job enthusiastically, and they also took on the duty of feeding their charge. There were about ten of them, and each brought him something from home to eat: bread, a handful of olives, dried figs, almonds, chickpeas, broad beans. They cooked the dried legumes in one of the roofless rooms, making a fire between two stones; and they had a great time.

The hunchback brought into his new palace his friend Achimelech, the beggar with the goitre, a person who had some fascination precisely because he was so repellent. The boys could touch the enormous growth that distorted his neck. Abraham came later, bringing along Jonathan, who had the mental age of a child and couldn't move by himself. The women came last; the men didn't want them, but accepted them because they were afraid of the witch.

With all the good will in the world, the boys would never have succeeded, relying solely on their own resources, in feeding six people, especially since Jesus didn't want them to steal from their homes, as they were ready and willing to do. For their charges there was only one course: to continue with their old activity, namely, begging. Until that moment they had asked for alms singly; now they learned the power of collective action.

When the six of them turned up at a door, a little collection of diverse monstrosities, with goitre, hunchback, game leg, drooling idiot's mouth, with the old sorceress's dishevelled appearance, and the horrid, toothless smile of the one-time harlot, people couldn't say no. They felt oppressed by that assemblage of deformities; they felt guilty because they were healthy and well-fed; and they gave.

But there were some who acted nonchalantly and refused to answer the pleas. Then the chorus of petitions was suddenly silent. Dour, looming, the six took their stand outside the door with the attitude of people ready to stay in the same place for hours, for the whole day, if necessary. The inhabitants of the house under siege would pay up, to make them go away.

I don't believe it was Jesus who suggested these terrorist tactics. In my opinion, the witch, accustomed to exploiting people's fears, invented new methods for the team of putting pressure on their fellow-humans. For a while the inhabitants of Nazareth suffered in silence; then the question was brought before the council of elders.

The Nazarenes had always considered a beggar an anonymous being, an almost symbolic vaguely human, figure, standing beneath the window or at the corner of a house, to whom you gave a coin, the one with the least value, to relieve your conscience. The beggar called down the Lord's blessing on his benefactor, which was surely worth more than the little coin he had received, then he disappeared again into the shadows. Nobody knew or wondered how the beggar lived, where he slept, what happened to him during the rest of the day. Now the group of beggars had the power to intimidate and oppress; they occupied a house, they were making a tacit claim to the rights of citizenship.

Everyone knew that, behind this upheaval of custom and tradition, enacted by the six beggars, there was the initiative of Jesus; but could a child's conduct decently be discussed in a serious meeting of elders. It would have been ridiculous. To talk about the new behaviour of the poor would have been dangerous: it was tantamout to recognizing it, giving a name to the threat it represented for the social order. The elders thought that at times it sufficed to keep your eyes closed while the danger disappeared. And so they discussed only the illegally occupied house. The proprietor presented a petition to regain free use of the building or what was left of it. It was decided to give the group of beggars two days in which to get out; if they refused, the house would be cleared by police forces.

I was preparing myself for some comical scenes, since the Nazareth police was represented by its sole component, old Hosea, who read out the king's decrees at street-corners, and rounded up the drunks at night when the taverns closed. Jesus robbed me of my entertainment. He agreed that property had to be respected, and he dissuaded his new friends from putting up their planned resistance. In two days, having chosen a patch of ground below the hill, where the land belonged to no one, all rocky, created by a flood, he built a shed of wood and stooks. Joseph supplied the poles, the planks, the tools; and I also lent a hand.

I was amazed that my master, who opposed his son's ventures, should now work for him.

'He's got himself into trouble with this idea he has of doing good to others. Jesus doesn't know how hard it is. Now he'll learn. But I don't want the lesson to be too severe: if his outcasts were to be dispensed suddenly, he would suffer too much.'

And he couldn't bear seeing the boy sad; sometimes when

Jesus was playing, he would suddenly stop and go to sit in a corner of the yard, out of sight, staying there, motionless, his eyes staring but not seeing, lost in unknown thoughts. Joseph would observe him, but he lacked the courage to ask the boy what was happening to him. He would give Jesus time, and after a while the boy would stir, his face would recover its liveliness, its ready smile. His father would shake his head, worried by those moments of contemplative absence, but reassured because they didn't last long.

The shed, which would later be completed with straw walls before the cold season, was ready within the established time, and the six moved in, carrying their stinking bundles, leaving their house in the city, as Jesus had told them to, in the state they had found it. In other words, they took the boy's order in a malicious sense, and they filled the place with all the refuse they could find: for enterprises of this sort they were even capable of working.

We saw them arrive at the shed, a little group of scarecrows, an array of troubles, a living reproach to the All-merciful, who had shown them little mercy. Joseph held his nose, and Jesus noticed.

Though Maria was always happy to share in her son's activities, not even she had intervened this time, because it was impossible for her to tolerate the stink of the six derelicts. She cooked for them, taking food from her own scant provender; but she couldn't stay near them. She was amazed that the boys, a couple of whom came from good families, weren't repelled by the bad smell.

'You just have to get over the first moment,' Jesus said, 'then you become used to it.'

Besides the convenience of not washing, the smell for the six mendicants was also a weapon and a simplification of their work. Anyone struck by it gave alms quickly, to send the stink elsewhere. Now, uniting their mephitic auras, the six gained another, irresistible element of pressure, when they took their stand at the door of a house. So they had more than one reason to oppose Jesus's demand that they wash every day. They hated water and didn't love nature: they were urban beggars. They also worked the outlying districts, but they stopped only at the more prosperous farms and never left the roads. They agreed to sleep on straw, but they were suspicious of grass, where stinging insects and snakes were concealed; they fled the rain that dissolved their armour of filth and transformed the hard roads into muddy sewers.

Sometimes they would go with Jesus and the boys into the hills, without sharing their interest in the animal life concealed, stirring gently in the green of the bushes and hedgerows, in the dust among the stones. They paid no attention to the stag beetles, the scarabs, the locusts, the garter snakes and the field mice. They looked out for moles, which are edible, hedgehogs and rabbits; and they observed the edges of the flocks, in case they could catch a stray lamb and hide it under their rags. They took great care that Jesus didn't catch them stealing.

They followed him on the hills around Nazareth because they enjoyed hearing him talk. I don't exactly know what the boy told them, but he never stopped chattering. He told them fables, parables, little narrative compositions very popular in the land of Israel; he would quote verses of Scripture. According to what I heard, he criticized the doctors of the Law, who are fonder of words than of their meaning, and the rich, who have no compassion for their neighbour, and soldiers, who like to kill. Once I followed him at a distance; his voice reached me every now and then.

He prevented Abraham the lame man from killing a snake that had slithered into the grass at their appearance.

'Can't you see how ugly it is?' Abraham said, to justify his action. 'It walks on its belly . . . '

' . . . and you, on your knees,' Jeremiah sniggered, and the others all burst out laughing.

Jesus said that nobody is responsible for the body he is given, but we're responsible for the use we make of it. He referred to a life after death, as a journey towards a happy land, where everyone will have a beautiful body. Naturally none of the beggars seriously believed in him, accustomed as they were to desire little and that immediately; but those words cheered them.

I looked at them as the group moved away: Jesus, with his blond hair, stood out among the boys. On his shoulder he carried the dove with the broken wing; the dogs scampered around him. The six followed, pushing one another and trading insults. The boy turned, and they looked sober, quiet as schoolchildren surprised by a look from the teacher.

Things between Jesus and his charges went wrong when he insisted they wash. In the first place, he said, the holy texts prescribe that we sit at table only after we have purified ourselves.

'That precept applies to those who have a table to sit at,' Achimelech ventured, and he meant that washing is all very well for the rich, who don't have to fear the cold; and, further, certain regulations, generally speaking, don't regard the poor. The man with the goitre argued that a considerable condition of filth is also a wealth not to be scattered; a blanket of various fats, stratified in the course of the years, is a defence against the elements, the harsh winter, against rain, wind, snow, and even against beatings. In his view, a back covered with dirt softened the blows of a stick.

Abraham was the first to give way. Jesus flattered him, made him laugh; he pleaded, invoked authority, he was comradely and brisk. In other words, he won him over, and on a certain morning the cripple was seen standing in the water of a stream that came down from the mountains and flowed near the shed. First Abraham was dressed, then naked, hopping to allay his revulsion and the tickling as the boys rubbed him with sand and brushes, gradually destroying the crust of dirt.

Next it was Achimelech's turn. Jeremiah ran off and stayed away for two days, because he couldn't bear the idea of displaying his hump naked and feeling outsiders touch it. Jonathan was too idiotic to try to resist: he cried like a child, then, under the water he burst into hysterical laughter.

That left the two women. Jesus turned to his mother for help. This time Maria overcame her repugnance, and with the assistance of Anna, the mother of one of the boys, she prepared to clean up Noemi and Esther. Naked, the two old women must have been an even more repulsive sight than when they were dressed, because when Maria came home, she vomited. And further, the witch hissed dire warnings at her, during the whole time she was in the water.

When the women, too, were finally washed, Jesus had a surprise for all. He had borrowed a table from home, which Joseph and I carried there. The boy invited the six to sit down, while he and his friends served the meal they had prepared in the deepest secrecy: bean soup with bread, roast rabbit, chick-pea mash, and a dram of wine.

Contrary to Jesus's expectations, there was no gaiety. The six sat there, embarrassed and writhing; they had washed, but they were wearing filthy rags. Awed, they were unable to enjoy their usual vulgar jokes. They felt strange. The gloomiest perhaps was Noemi the witch: as a rule her hair flew around her head, a wispy, wild crown. Now, wet, it stuck to her skull; and the old woman, having lost her crest, seemed dwarfed. She didn't say a word during the supper, and I realized she was preparing her revenge, ready to equal and, if possible, overcome Jesus's influence with her own.

The next morning, when the boy ran out to the place as usual, he found no one there. Defeated by their cleanliness and frightened by the proper behaviour he wanted to impose on them, the six had run off, returning to their life of uncontrolled individualism. As old Esther had grumbled some days before, they had to save themselves in time: washing was only the first step, next would come work and the synagogue, different aspects of the same prison.

Jesus was deeply pained. He couldn't understand why his rehabilitation plan had broken down. As soon as I tried to explain it to him, he immediately understood and blamed himself. 'I shouldn't have started,' he said, 'I'm still too little,' as if he saw his life devoted, professionally, to that task of rescuing the lost, gathering up those who were left behind.

Joseph was glad it had ended like this, but he was careful to contain himself, so his son wouldn't be aware of his father's relief. We demolished the shed and carried home the poles and the planks.

I thought we had rid ourselves once and for all of Jesus's derelicts; but one morning we found the idiot lying in the middle of the yard, unconscious. There was a wound on his brow. Jesus rushed out to care for him. Maria also went out, and together we laid him on a little cot in my shed.

The wound wasn't serious. Jonathan came to, stared at us with his dazed eyes, childishly happy that someone was looking after him. He saw Jesus and happily smiled at him. As a rule he spoke in a confused way; now, stunned by the blow on the head, he was totally incomprehensible. We never learned what had happened to him. Separated from his usual guardian, Abraham the cripple, he had no other recourse but to come to

Jesus. He had dragged himself into the yard and there had fainted.

He wasn't someone who could go around by himself, even when he had recovered. Jesus went to his father, asking him to allow Jonathan to stay with us.

'He's as innocent as a child,' Jesus said, 'would you shut the door on a child?'

Joseph hesitated, and then Jesus found the right argument: he convinced his father, and taught me that lack of charity is almost always caused by scant imagination.

'Think, if you were in his place,' the boy said, 'incapable of looking ahead, exposed to every danger. Everything is frightening; you don't even know how to beg, or you don't dare to . . .'

It was hard for his father to see himself as a creature so wanting in contacts with the world and the time. Jesus adjusted his aim: 'Think if it were me. Think of me when I was six years old. I have left the house and got lost. I am weeping at a street-corner. Wouldn't you be happy if someone took me by the hand and led me to his house?'

Joseph said that Jonathan could stay and became quite fond of him. Jesus spoke to the idiot as if he could understand. His father said nothing to him, but took him food and sat beside him for a long time in the evening, so that Jonathan could fall peacefully asleep. Jesus didn't see him, for he was already asleep at that hour. I saw him. Once I called Maria and took her, silently, to look at her husband performing his act of charity. She pressed my arm, as she leaned on it: it was a way of thanking me without words.

A month went by. Abraham the cripple turned up in our yard and reclaimed the idiot as if Jonathan were his property. Jonathan hesitated, torn between his former subjection, which impelled him towards his comrade, and the new affection that held him with us.

Angrily Joseph seized a hammer on the bench and was preparing to drive away the intruder. But Jesus had learned the lesson: 'We'll let him choose,' he said. Abraham was made to step back as far as the gate, so he and we would be the same distance from the idiot. Both sides were silenced. Jonathan, in the middle, was groaning in the effort of deciding. He headed towards us, then stopped, turned back, and running across the yard, went and hid his head against the cripple's shoulder. Abraham gave us a triumphant sneer, and took him away.

Jesus heaved a deep sigh. I cursed. And Joseph burst into tears, as if a son had been taken from him.

XIV

Jesus fell ill. Joseph sat up with him, disputing with Maria the task of caring for the boy. He fanned him, wiped his face, flushed and feverish, with a damp cloth. Perhaps he reproached himself for not having loved him enough.

One night he felt that the fever was rising. Jesus's face was swollen; he was delirious. My master went to fetch Tobias, the doctor, who arrived, prescribed a blood-letting, asked and was given a silver half-shekel in payment for the call, and went home to resume his interrupted sleep.

I was about to run for Baruch, who sells cures in the square, shaves beards, cuts hair, and lets blood; but Maria objected. No one, she insisted, was to shed Jesus's blood. She was horrified at the thought that her son should undergo the normal trials of the flesh; she was in despair when he came home blood-stained from brawls with his companions. She looked on his body as something precious, almost sacred. She kept his hair, every time she trimmed it, the parings of his nails, the hairs that fell from his eyelashes, as if nothing of him should be lost.

She opposed the blood-letting with the determination she brought to all grave decisions; she wept, became desperate, and so agitated that my master gave in. He held her in his arms. 'What if he dies?' he asked, in a stifled voice.

Maria answered softly: 'Him? Now? From a child's disease? That's impossible.'

Her assurance was dumbfounding: her worry and her sleepless nights had clouded her judgement. At times like that a mother never really knows what she is saying.

Even without the blood-letting Jesus recovered. One night he sank into a deep sleep, and the next morning he woke without any fever. He thanked them both, his father and his mother, for their care of him. He thanked me, too, though I had done very little.

He was completely well in a couple of days and wanted to get up. 'Rise, Jesus,' he said to himself, joking: 'Rise and walk.' His mother insisted he stay in bed a while yet. Joseph came in from the shop to take over from his wife and to keep the boy company.

In the months after he got well, Jesus grew a palm taller, and achieved a man's height. He grew furiously, and lost weight. He was twelve years old now. His father established a kind of complicity with him, treating him as an adult. 'We men,' he would say. The boy, who was going through that stage when your father is an enemy, grew even closer to Maria, disputing her affection with her husband. And yet he was submissive to his father, obeying him and showing him respect.

The time had come, according to my master, when the boy should be instructed in certain aspects of life. Joseph wanted to talk to him himself, so that love and sex wouldn't be crudely revealed to him by some older companion.

In the presence of women Jesus wasn't shy, but reserved, careful not to look at them, not to seem in any way indiscreet. In his day Joseph had behaved differently: at twelve he used to crouch in the ditches, in the grass, to admire from a favourable perspective the legs of the girls who came along the road, or else he and the other boys would hide and spy on the serving maids doing the washing at the trough, their breasts bouncing inside their tunics. In that respect Jesus seemed calmer; even as a child, when his mother took him to the synagogue and the women went into ecstasies over his beauty, he had never displayed pleasure or annoyance, but rather a polite indifference.

Joseph took his son out for a walk towards the countryside, at sunset. He began a roundabout discourse; he said that the reality of life is revealed little by little, that certain curiosities of ours are satisfied as we grow up. 'You, too, must be curious to know certain things,' he went on, 'how babies are born, for example.'

'No,' Jesus said calmly.

'You're not curious?' Joseph asked, his embarrassment increasing by the moment.

'No, because I know how babies are born; like puppies, like lambs, like kittens: from their mothers' belly.'

'How do you know that?'

'Everybody knows these things. You just have to read Scriptures with a bit of attention.'

Joseph took another tack. 'Soon,' he said, 'in a year, perhaps, you'll discover that we men are interested in girls . . . '

'I like them already,' Jesus said, smiling as if to reassure Joseph.

'You never look at them,' Joseph grumbled, somewhat humiliated.

'But I see them. If you want, I'll describe one to you,' and he began, as if in fun, to describe the face and the figure of a woman, so precisely that my master recognized her immediately as Daniel's Maria. To Joseph it seemed that the choice of subject betrayed a sly intention. But after the first woman, Jesus described a second, with the same abundance of details, and then a third; and Joseph didn't fail to recognize them either.

Jesus didn't hesitate before female forms or before words, either. He didn't say womb, the way timid narrators do; he said belly. And he said breasts, not bosom. Joseph blushed: then he realized that the boy was talking in this way out of love of precision, without euphemisms and without smirks: the same straightforward manner in which he would have described a horse or a sunset.

Jesus hesitated when his father asked him about a girl who lived in our street, directly opposite the yard. He said she was tall for her age, black-haired, and she laughed in a special way, a gurgling laughter; and that was all he said. Joseph recognized the symptoms: this was not the description of a person but of a feeling, vague, undefined, just coming into existence. He didn't ask anything further. For that matter, a few months later he noticed that, once his passion for nomenclature had passed, Jesus was filled with a new modesty and referred only in paraphrases to certain parts of the body, especially the female body.

In Joseph's opinion, the conversation was growing too intimate; and as a good father, he directed it towards other subjects. Perhaps Jesus had displayed this calm mastery of the matter in order to provoke his father: ever since his childhood he had been allowed to answer back, and the boy had become a true interlocutor.

'In other words,' Joseph said, to conclude, 'you aren't indifferent to women.'

'On the contrary, I love them. How could I help but love women, when they make up half of the human race?'

Joseph felt that this statement referred to a feeling different from the one he meant, but he had no doubt of the boy's sincerity.

Jesus never told a lie; he didn't even employ those innocuous falsehoods that smooth rough corners and make dealings with other people easier. Through an association of ideas that wasn't clear even to him, my master began a lecture on how the truth was to be respected in substantial matters and on how convenient little lies, in his view, were not only innocent but in some cases opportune and even necessary. He spoke of white lies, and Jesus rejected them as useless; of lies or tricks in love and war, and Jesus didn't understand; finally he thought he had found the decisive argument: 'You would surely tell a lie to save your life,' Joseph said to him.

Jesus thought it over and answered: 'I'm afraid not,' in a low voice, as if he were sorry to disappoint his father.

They spoke no more. A feeling of sadness had filled them, and they headed for home, in the falling darkness, comforted by the thought of food, the warm, lighted room. He'll learn, Joseph thought, convinced that telling lies at the right time and place is an art that doesn't offend the Lord. What Jesus was thinking I couldn't say, because, while I knew my master well, I couldn't always manage to understand the boy, not even when he spoke clearly. True, as they grow up, they change and resemble us in the end, but at that time Jesus seemed to me different from me and from his companions, even if he did everything he could to seem like other people. A boy who won't tell a lie not even to avoid punishment, in my opinion, isn't normal. If a man were to behave like that, I'd consider him a danger, to himself and to others.

His obsession with defending animals, usually fairly badly treated in Israel, also exasperated his father, because when Jesus was fighting the oppressors of the weak, he would lose all sense of proportion. When he caught boys breaking a dog's tail, coating a bird's wings with pitch, or sticking a straw into a bumblebee's behind, the boy would go wild. He would even fight grownups, if necessary. Joshua the coal-burner came to the house to complain that Joseph's son had butted him in the stomach and knocked him to the ground, only because the boy had seen him beating an ass.

Summoned to explain his behaviour, Jesus apologized for having hit Joshua, but insisted it had been necessary because the ass had nobody to defend him and there was no other way to show the coal-burner he was making a mistake.

'What was the mistake you wanted to show me?' Joshua asked.

'The idea that an ass gains strength from being beaten. If you whip him and he won't move, the only solution is to lighten the weight he is carrying.'

The man went off grumbling and describing what he would do to Jesus, if the boys were his, as the ass was his.

Joseph didn't understand, either. 'What was it all about? Asses have been beaten, to make them move, ever since the world began.'

'And what if they can't keep going, like Joshua's?'

'What of it? Jackasses don't have souls.'

'I don't know,' Jesus replied, 'but anyone can see that they suffer.'

Joseph tackled the matter from a different angle: 'You mustn't interfere: the ass belongs to him and he can do whatever he wants with it.'

At that moment the boy didn't know what to answer. Mentally, he reviewed the scripture and found nothing on the subject of maltreated animals. Joseph wanted to strengthen his advantage. 'Isn't there some verse of the Law,' he asked, 'that says you're right?' And he smiled.

'No,' Jesus admitted.

'In that case,' his father went on, ironically, 'the Law will have to be changed.' His tone was that of someone making an inconceivable suggestion: that night should become day, or asses should fly.

'Yes,' Jesus said, gravely.

Then Joseph became angry. He made as if to rend his garments, and said: 'Who do you think you are, you little monster of pride? Presumptuous. Irreverent. Twelve years old, and you want to change the world?'

‘Yes,’ Jesus said again, and his father cried that the boy was a sinner, and made him stand in a corner, as a penance.

Maria came into the room, summoned by her husband’s agitated voice. Joseph told her what had happened, and he repeated, indignantly: ‘You know what he says? That he wants to change the world? The world we live in doesn’t suit him.’

Maria looked at him and said in that calm voice of hers, which lent such intensity to her words: ‘And does it suit you, the world we live in?’

‘I make do,’ Joseph answered, with irony. ‘Not being as presumptuous as he is, I know I can’t change it.’

Joseph loathed the idea of change, the eagerness for novelty that torments the young. Even when he was eighteen, his breaches of the moral code had respected, as far as possible, traditional customs and the social order: he stayed away from wives and virgins, and sinned with widows, who were independent. Now it seemed to him that paternal authority was being threatened, at least in his house; and, somewhat bewildered, he opposed this betrayal.

He no longer began his preaching to his son with the words ‘In my time . . . ’ because Jesus would point out to him that times had changed; but Joseph would protest when Maria took her son’s side and attempted to save him from punishment.

One evening Jesus was ordered to go without supper, because he had answered his father disrespectfully. Joseph had scolded him because instead of helping in the shop, the boy ran off with his friends to the hills. For the occasion my master had decided to sing the praises of work, and he began by quoting the Lord’s words on expelling Adam from the Earthly Paradise: ‘In the sweat of thy face shalt thou eat bread . . . ’

‘ . . . and dried figs,’ Jesus had added, interrupting him and referring to what, accompanied by a bit of milk, was their regular meal almost every evening.

Later Maria had gone into her son’s room with a tray. On it was a bowl of milk and a piece of bread, to feed him in secret. ‘I am being punished,’ he said, ‘and this time I deserve it. Those words escaped me, but I shouldn’t have said them. It sounded as if I were complaining of our poverty, blaming him for it . . . ’

Maria insisted, but the boy was firm. The sound of their words reached Joseph, who was coming to tell Jesus he was forgiven and could return to the table. My master became angry with Maria. 'There,' he said, 'you always try to undo my efforts to give the child some education. You're always there to console him, to take his side against me. So you teach him to stand up to me, and you destroy my authority. Does going to bed without supper seem such a harsh punishment to you? In my day a boy who behaved the way he did would have been lashed with a bullwhip. I'm easy-going and to you I seem severe. A trifling punishment, if I inflict it, seems to you cruel . . . '

She apologized. 'A growing boy, on the move from morning till night, can't be left without food,' she said.

Joseph continued his accusations. 'When you smile at what I'm saying to him, my reproaches lose any meaning; I punish him, and you forgive him. I train him to recognize his mistakes, and you pass over them. Who is the head of this household, you or me?'

Joseph left the house, after his tirade, but he didn't have the money to go to the tavern as he would have done in the past. He walked through the streets which the descending night had emptied, and he inwardly bemoaned his fate. He had become resigned to Maria's illness, that strange illness which meant that she was perfectly well until he asked her to act like a wife; he could put up with chastity, even with the secondary role he realized he was playing in the family. But the memory of the unknown man, with whom Maria had conceived her son, still tortured him. She had never spoken of it since then; not a single word had ever escaped her.

Joseph came home, sat down beside me in the yard, on the front step of my shed. 'You . . . ' He suddenly said to me. 'Did you ever figure out who it was?'

I knew immediately what he was talking about, and I shook my head. I remembered he had asked me much the same question one night, more than ten years before. Joseph was silent for a long time, then he went on: 'You remember Tamar? And Dorothea? And the girls of Bethlehem, who said goodbye to me, waving their veils and handkerchiefs from the windows? And my handsome horse: remember him? Maybe you also remember what I said then: that I didn't want to fall in love. Was I right, or not? Look how I've shrivelled up. The great life is over, and I don't know why I stay in this world . . . '

'You have Maria,' I said, to console him, 'and little Jesus . . . '

'What does Jesus matter to me?' he burst out. 'When he obeys me, I feel he's making fun of me. If he listens to me, I can see his mind is on other things. You know that way he has of looking at you, with a little smile, as if he knew everything and feels sorry for you? I hate him at those moments. I'd like to leave him here with his mother and go off by myself, back to Egypt.'

For a moment he returned in his thoughts to the memories of his exile, then he shrugged and continued: 'You say I have Maria, and you don't realize that she's the one who has me. I come in handy for her. She uses me, except as a husband . . . As for her, she belongs to Jesus, not to me. Who am I, after all? Not a father, not a husband. They'd have to invent a new word for me, meaning a joke of a husband, a fake father, a genuine fool . . . '

I really didn't know what to say to him, so I kept silent. Joseph stood up, gave a stone a kick, and withdrew into the house. That night he slept in a corner of the shop, on the sawdust, as he did sometimes, when he could no longer bear the closeness of a beautiful woman lying in the same room with him. On these occasions Maria was hurt, but naturally she was aware of what her husband was suffering, and she didn't say a word.

Jesus realized at once when his father had slept in the shop, and not daring to ask Joseph the reason, he would fire questions at his mother. What could poor Maria answer him? She said that perhaps Joseph had come home late and hadn't come up to the bedroom for fear of waking her. The next time, since Jesus knew that the two of them had gone to bed at the same time, one upstairs and one down, this answer no longer worked. Maria groped desperately; like her son, she was incapable of telling lies.

'You know, but you don't want to tell me,' Jesus concluded. 'Can I ask him?'

'No, no,' Maria beseeched him. 'It's best not to.'

The next day Jesus saw his father with a long face and stayed in the shop to help him, considerate and affectionate. Sensing the boy's good intentions, Joseph was moved. Jesus was no star pupil, nor was he a model of good conduct; but he had a heart. For that matter, my master was very fond of him: he scolded him, and punished him, because that is part of a father's duty.

XV

Far from becoming a carpenter, as his father would have liked, or a rabbi, as his mother dreamed, Jesus – in my view – sometimes seemed destined to be a conjuror, one of those men who earn their living by performing tricks, playing in the squares of Galilee on market days. He indulged his fondness for jokes only rarely, because they made his father angry; but when he did them, he was really skilled. Joseph would reach for a nail he had left on the bench, and it would vanish. He would hunt for it on the floor, and Jesus would help him, also bending over. Then, straightening up, they saw the nail exactly where it had been before. On his father's good-humoured days, Jesus would make even his plate disappear, as Joseph was eating from it.

One evening there was nothing for supper but a few shelled beans. Maria set the dish in the centre of the table, so that they could all help themselves. She felt a bit ashamed, because the beans were really few, perhaps two dozen in all. Still, they began eating. As they ate the beans, the same beans would reappear in the dish, which was never empty. Joseph realized that Jesus, when he reached out to take a bean, was concealing some others in his hand, so when he took one, he would leave three or four in its place.

He seized the boy's wrist as Jesus was stretching his right hand towards the dish. 'Open your fingers,' he commanded, triumphantly. The boy unclenched his hand: it was empty. He was too sharp for Joseph; he had sensed the moment when his father would act, and he had arranged to fool him.

'You see?' Maria said, pleased.

'All right,' Joseph admitted, as he was actually enjoying himself, 'he beat me. I don't care how he works his tricks, but

I'd like to know where he got the beans.'

'He didn't steal them,' Maria declared, hastening to the boy's defence.

'I know he's not a thief, but he got them somewhere, didn't he?' Joseph said, as Maria inadvertently denied the charge, shaking her head. And Joseph added, in an ironic tone: 'I understand: you think your son works miracles: the multiplication of the beans. If they were gold pieces, at least . . . '

'I don't feel any need for gold pieces,' she said, to change the subject. And if that was her aim, she succeeded perfectly.

'Maybe you don't, but I'd be quite happy to see a sack of gold.' And Joseph abandoned himself to the dream of wealth, which was one of his favourite dreams. He went into great detail about what he would do and what he would buy, if he had plenty of money. A saddle-horse, to begin with. And so he forgot his investigation into the source of the beans he was eating.

I, on the contrary, didn't forget, but try as I would, I never managed to find out which garden Jesus had taken them from. There were a lot, enough for supper; and some were even set aside for the next day.

Unfortunately, as Joseph said, they weren't gold pieces; a bit of money in the house would have come in handy also against the expenses that had to be faced for the pilgrimage to Jerusalem. Jesus was twelve years old, and it was time he went to the temple. The family decided they would travel as cheaply as possible, on foot, naturally, and with their belongings on their backs, because the ass had long since been sold. After more than ten years, Maria recognized the places along the road; and at a certain point she insisted they go out of their way, to avoid the sight of the crosses that, as she remembered, had stood just a little farther on. Ever since the time when, as they were going to Bethlehem and she was carrying Jesus, she had come upon the four crucified men, she had felt a horror of the cross. The others knew of this weakness of hers and took care that nothing should suggest the idea to her.

She had only to see a couple of twigs crossed or a sign like the Greek letter X scrawled with chalk on a shipment of wood, and Maria would turn pale and look away.

When we came to our stopping place, we realized that Jesus was missing. The boy was always running ahead, or dawdling, straying beyond the road to explore, to left and right; and we had lost track of him. He joined us a little later, running. Joseph took him close to the fire; and seeing him very pale and upset, he guessed the reason for the boy's absence: 'You went to see the crucified men,' he whispered.

'There were three of them,' the boy confirmed.

'Why are you always poking around where you shouldn't be? You saw that we went out of our way to avoid them.'

'I want to see everything,' Jesus said, in a tone of voice that tried in vain to sound steady, grown up. He was trembling, and his teeth chattered.

'Don't tell your mother, in any case.'

Jesus promised, and he kept his word.

When we reached Jerusalem, we camped outside the walls, to save money, and also because there were no lodgings to be found in the city. We were taken into the tent of the Nazareth wagon-owner as his guests; he was the father of Joel, the young man with smelly feet. The man was a good friend of Joseph's; his tent was huge, and he had brought it there on a light wagon, drawn by mules. We settled in comfortably. Maria was especially pleased because she could go off with our host's wife to the section set aside for the women, divided from the general area by a hempen curtain.

The next morning we went up to the temple, which was as vast as a palace, with courtyards and colonnades. My master and his wife performed their devotions, offered a sacrifice, and we all went back to the tent. There we realized that Jesus was no longer with us. These things happen: the father thinks the boy's with his mother, and vice versa, and when the parents meet, they see he's missing.

'We've lost him,' Maria said, weeping.

'He's the one who decided to lose us,' Joseph guessed. 'He must be enjoying himself hugely, going around in such a big city by himself. All right, I'll go and look for him,' he added, because Maria wouldn't stop crying.

He roamed the streets of Jerusalem all day, but Jesus wasn't to be found.

'He'll turn up on the third day,' I said to Maria, to console her. 'That's what he always does.'

I also searched the lower city, where a boy on his own really can be lost, but in vain. And then, the evening of the third day,

Joseph came back to the tent with a boy. He had found him in the temple.

Maria embraced Jesus, hugging him so hard she almost hurt him. Finally a word of reproach escaped her: 'Where have you been, son? We searched all over for you . . . Why did you cause us so much distress?'

Jesus murmured his usual, disagreeable answer, keeping his distance from his mother, to the effect that he had to tend to his own business and that he was big enough to go around by himself.

Joseph impetuously gave him a slap. 'Is that the proper way to answer your mother?'

Jesus didn't let his father have the final word. 'I don't know,' he said, 'the proper way to answer my mother. But that's the way I answered her.' And he gained a second slap.

Maria emitted a moan, as if she had received the blows; her eyes filled with tears.

When evening came, husband and wife went off to talk between themselves, seated on the grass among the bushes that grew in the lee of the walls.

'Are you sure you love me?' Joseph asked her. The sons of Israel don't often talk this way; discussing private feelings is considered rather useless, and somehow indecorous. If anything, they use scriptural phrases, with their talk of hearts leaping like stags, or of being weary unto death.

'You know I do,' Maria replied. 'I've never loved any man but you.' Her voice was hesitant, anxious: Maria wanted him to believe her.

'Yes,' Joseph said. 'And I have loved - and love - only you.'

He stretched out on the grass and put his head in her lap; Maria stroked his hair. 'I owe you great gratitude,' she said. 'You took me into your house, you accepted the child, you never asked of me more than I could give you. Few men - perhaps no man - would have been able to love a woman that much.'

He laughed. 'I couldn't argue. It was take it or leave it. You know I had never loved before; I would have done anything for you.'

'Poor Joseph,' Maria said, 'you could be happy, and instead, look at the life I've forced you to lead.'

These were more or less the words Dorothea had spoken on

bidding a final goodbye to my master; but how different Maria's tone was, and how much affection there was in her meaning.

'What do I have to complain of?' Joseph said. 'I have rewards: you, the boy. But you . . . you could really have hoped for a better life.'

'What do I have to complain of?' Maria repeated his words, smiling.

'When a man's young,' Joseph went on, 'he always dreams of becoming important or of accumulating a lot of money. I soon gave up such dreams. There's a special happiness also in being ordinary people, the same as everybody else. In a few years nobody will talk about us, except our son, and his children. Then more time will go by, and we'll be completely forgotten, as if we had never existed. This is the fate of everyone, or almost everyone, and it doesn't seem a bad fate to me. What do you think about it?'

'I don't have any ambitions,' Maria said. 'Women can't have any.'

The air was cooling as the sun began to set.

'Tell me when I do something wrong with the boy,' he begged her.

'Don't worry. Jesus knows you love him. Maybe I'm wrong sometimes, too. It's so hard to be mothers and fathers.'

My master had become a very fine carpenter. He had turned over to me that part of the job that required only physical labour, like cutting the logs and dressing them. I roughed out the plough, the yokes, the wagons. Joseph dealt with furniture, the tables and chests and chairs, and he warded off boredom by looking for new solutions. He built some chairs that fitted the body more comfortably, with the back curved and the seat hollow; stools that could be folded when not used; tables that could be extended or shortened as required.

These jobs were not paid as well as they should have been, and Joseph spent lots of time on them, chiefly out of love for his craft. The boy helped him.

Jesus also understood his mother's work, constant and silent, beginning all over again every day: washing tunics that would soon be dirty once more, sweeping rooms that would fill with dust a little later. Though no one ordered him to do it, he would go out to fetch water at the well or from the spring at the corner of the road, where it flowed always and was more fresh.

Maria would thank him, but she didn't want him to perform other household chores, sweeping the floor or grinding the grain, for example. 'That's my job,' she would say, 'you have other things to think about.' Perhaps she thought that Jesus should conceive great ideas instead of bothering with humble, everyday tasks. Or she may simply have been thinking that a man should be spared woman's work.

It was at this time that Joseph conceived the invention which is, after all, the reason why I have narrated his life, so that he will not be forgotten.

Back in Bethlehem, after the child's birth, since he had nothing to do, he would often climb up the hill to talk with our friends the shepherds. He saw them crouch down on their heels, to do the milking. The effort of pulling on the teats was complicated by the problem of holding between their knees the bucket to be filled.

In Nazareth Joseph often went for a walk outside the walls, after a day's work. Flocks were to be seen everywhere, large and small, scattered over the hills and through the meadows. At sunset the shepherds did the milking, and Joseph kept thinking how uncomfortable their position was as they worked.

One day he made a strange contraption: a stool with a single leg. I was puzzled when I looked at his invention: from a circular wooden seat, a supporting leg, only one, extended, in the centre. A strip of leather allowed you to sling the stool over your shoulder: so the seat stuck to your body, leaving your hands free. In this way, the milkers seemed to have a third leg, or a stiff tail that, pressed against the ground, supported them.

It didn't take me long to figure out how useful this stool would be for milkers. I also realized how original it was: it was something new, a genuine invention. Nowadays, when a thing's in use far and wide, people forget who its inventor was. This is what happens with little, valuable inventions that seem to have sprung up on their own; so it is only right to give Joseph the credit due him.

Joseph may not have been a great man; he didn't lead armies or rule over his people, but he was an excellent carpenter, a craftsman of genius. His milking-stool is so simple that it seems to have existed always, and surely no change could improve it: a sign that, big or little, it is a true invention.

We made a number of stools for the shepherds in the area, but one day, when we went to the slopes of Carmel to load some logs, we saw that there, too, men were milking their sheep with Joseph's stool tied to their backs. And those weren't stools we had made. The invention had spread fast. We had hoped it would bring in great profits; on the contrary, it wasn't going to make us rich.

'Too bad,' I said.

'Why? There are some things that should belong to everybody, freely.'

From the top of the pile of logs on the wagon we looked down at the dense, woolly clumps of sheep, gathered together for the night. Their colour darkened in the twilight. As we passed close to one of these animal assemblies, the sweetish smell of the milk and the smell of damp fleece made us yearn to be home soon. But, in tacit agreement, we lingered.

The sun floated another moment, fiery red, on the jagged line of the hill, then it set. The shepherds lighted fires, to cook their barley meal.

'I want you to help Maria,' Joseph said, 'when I'm gone.'

I protested: 'Why, what are you thinking of? You're ten years younger than I am.'

He smiled: 'Only in case I die before you, naturally. The boy is grown now; he'll work. I worry about him for another reason: he doesn't like the world the way it is. And you know what happens to someone who wants to change the world on his own: if he's lucky, he ends up in prison. Jesus is too impulsive; he has no idea of prudence. These are restless times: if somebody doesn't restrain him, I'm sure he'll come to a bad end.'

He begged me to keep an eye on the boy, to get him out of the troubles in which, his father felt, he would inevitably get himself involved.

Joseph wasn't sad. He insisted we stop along the way for a glass of wine at a tavern, and he recalled, with me, our past adventures. He laughed and slapped me on the back. I don't know why, but this gaiety disturbed me more than his words.

Jesus, too, sharp-eyed as he was, sensed something in

Joseph's face, behind his usual smile. The next day the boy stayed at his side from morning till evening, helping out in the shop. I heard them laugh together, something I hadn't heard since Jesus was a child.

The morning after that my master came down to work, but he slumped down between the bench and the wall, first to his knees, then prone, in the sawdust. Joseph didn't cry out, but as if she had seen him from the well where she was drawing water, at a great distance and through the wall, Maria came running: the cry we heard was Maria's. With her help I carried the master to the upper room and laid him on the bed.

Joseph was paralyzed; he could move only his right hand, but that was enough to let him give us some little signals, that we tried to interpret; he couldn't speak, but he smiled. He smiled at us always, for all the time that his life still lasted. As if his smile forced them, Maria and Jesus, in his presence, avoided saddening him with tears. Every now and then Maria would go off, to a corner of the yard, and moan, whimpering like a little whipped dog. Jesus would vanish behind the house, towards the hill.

I also often went up to visit our patient. There, I said to him in my mind, now you are allowed in the marriage bed, poor Joseph, after sleeping on the ground all these years. But you lie there alone, like a widower.

It wasn't true. I realized that Maria, now that her husband's body no longer frightened or repelled her, would stretch out at night beside him, sleeping when he slept and staying awake when he was awake. She stroked him and kissed him; I'm sure my master sensed those contacts and the feeling that inspired them.

One evening he seemed to improve. He managed to utter one word: Maria. She rushed to him, but he didn't speak again: he looked at her. He looked at her, as if he were offering her his soul.

Later Jesus came to his side. To him, too, my master managed to say a few last words. 'Don't get married,' he whispered, moving one eyelid in a brief wink. Jesus smiled and winked back.

Maria hadn't heard him, but if she had, she would have understood, as I had understood, that those words didn't contradict the love her husband bore her.

Joseph died early in the morning. He stirred from a restless sleep, shuddered, murmured another word that none of us was able to understand. He heaved a deep sigh and closed his eyes.

Maria moaned, kneeling on the floor, like someone who doesn't want to be consoled; and Jesus wept. I had never seen him cry; not even when he used to fall down and hurt himself, not even when other boys had hit him; now the tears flowed down his cheeks. I sought some words to comfort him: 'He was a just man,' I said, and nothing else.

This happened last year, at this season.